By the time we'd gotten all the way to the bottom of the cliff, the rain and wind were so strong that it looked as if the air was full of blowing smoke. How would we ever find a kitten in this?

"Listen!" said Lisa.

There was a tiny, ti... just hear it on the wind.

"Where's it coming from?" Abby asked.

"There," said Lisa, pointing. We ran down the beach and stood below a little chink in the rocks—not even a cave, really—that was about eight feet above our heads.

"Sebastian!" yelled Molly.

"Mew!" We could just see his little face, peeking out over the edge above us.

Read these books in
THE ANIMAL RESCUE SQUAD
series:

And look for more coming your way soon!

THE ANIMAL RESCUE SQUAD™

#1

Kitten Alert!

by Ellen Weiss
and Mel Friedman

BULLSEYE BOOKS

Random House 🏠 New York

For Nora, saver of strays

A BULLSEYE BOOK PUBLISHED BY RANDOM HOUSE, INC.

Copyright © 1995 by Ellen Weiss and Mel Friedman
Cover design by Fabia Wargin Design and Creative Media
Applications, Inc. All rights reserved under International and
Pan-American Copyright Conventions. Published in the United States
by Random House, Inc., New York, and simultaneously in Canada by
Random House of Canada Limited, Toronto.

Library of Congress Catalog Card Number: 94-71249
ISBN: 0-679-85865-2
RL: 3.2

First Bullseye Books edition: June 1995

Manufactured in the United States of America   10 9 8 7 6 5 4 3 2 1

THE ANIMAL RESCUE SQUAD is a trademark of Random House, Inc.

Contents

How It Started

So there I was, practicing my tuba. Now, you might think that's funny, an eleven-year-old girl practicing the tuba. Everybody does. But it's not funny. It's hard. You have to hold up this really heavy instrument in just the right position on the chair in front of you, and then you have to buzz your lips, hard, into the mouthpiece. After you practice a while, this makes a really attractive red circle all around your mouth. And if you don't sound like a moose with a toothache, you're doing well. Plus, people make fun of you. And my dogs hate it. They hide when they see me take it out of the case.

But anyhow, I was practicing my tuba, and then the phone rang downstairs.

"Eliza!" yelled my mother. "It's for you!"

"Do you know who it is?" I shouted, not wanting to untangle myself from my tuba unless it was really important.

"She didn't say. I think it's Lisa."

"Okay, I'm coming," I called down. For Lisa, I would definitely stop practicing.

I guess before we get any deeper into this story I should tell you who I am. My name is Eliza Spain. I am very tall and skinny—in fact, I'm the tallest person in my class. I'm also the oldest person in my class, because my birthday is January 2, and in my city, which is Dormouth, Massachusetts, you have to be five by January 1 to start kindergarten. No exceptions. As if having always been the tallest, skinniest, and oldest person wasn't bad enough, I also wear really, really thick glasses. They make my eyes look all big and funny when you look at me. Plus, I've got frizzy dirty-blond hair that's supposed to stay in a ponytail, but it doesn't. I have my dad's exact hair.

I try not to let all these things get to me, but I can't help it. They do. I worry about my looks. I worry about everything. I think I'm what people call a sensitive type. This, of course, worries me. I don't want to be a sensitive, timid, careful type. I want to be the strong, cheerful type. I want to be a bold leader. I'm not the person who says, "Hey, let's go swing on that rope over that lake"—

I'm the person who says, "Um, I think I have to go do my homework now."

One thing that's very good about me, though, is that I really, really love and care about animals. I guess I got it from my mom— she's a veterinarian. We have three dogs. Their names are Big, Little, and Archie, and they are all strays I brought home. Big is red and flop-eared and weighs 105 pounds. Little is black, weighs 12 pounds, and sings. Archie is just a pain. But we love him. (Well, my dad doesn't love him that much.)

It's because I love animals so much that I first had the idea for the Animal Rescue Squad. Of course, that wasn't till much later. This is the story of how it all started. I suppose it really began with that phone call.

It was, in fact, Lisa on the phone. Lisa Ho, one of my very best friends.

"Are you coming?" she said.

"Coming where?"

"You forgot. I knew you would, you punk. We're going out to sell magazines today, remember?"

I fell into the chair, just missing the part where Archie had chewed the stuffing out and the spring was poking through. Little immediately hopped onto my lap.

"Oh, no!" I moaned. "I did forget. I have to

finish practicing, and I have to do my home-work, and—"

"And you have to sell magazines with Molly and me," Lisa finished. "It's important, Eliza. There won't be a fifth-grade trip to New York unless we get out there and sell some subscriptions. We'll just go out for an hour."

I knew she was right. We—the fifth grade—had to raise two thousand dollars, or we wouldn't be going anywhere. "Okay," I agreed. "An hour."

"We'll meet you on the corner," said Lisa. "Five minutes." It's handy that she lives right around the corner from me, and Molly is just two blocks away, on Neptune Street.

And so, five minutes later, there was Lisa, waiting for me on the corner. Today Lisa had her black hair in that neat kind of Chinese braid her grandmother makes. When she lets it down, which is only once in a while, it reaches to her waist. "It's a blessing and a curse," she told me once. "I like it and every-thing, but it's so hard to take care of, and it's hot in the summer. But I've never cut it, not once. I've invested so many years in it, I just can't do it. I'd *die* if I cut my hair." Lisa's a lit-tle dramatic. Today, she was wearing a black sweatshirt with a lightning bolt on it, jeans with a huge rip in the knee, and sparkly red sneakers.

Molly got to the corner a minute later. Molly Penrose, my oldest friend in the world (since our mothers shared a hospital room when we were born), is just about the exact opposite of Lisa. She has short, straight brown hair, pink cheeks, and wire-rimmed glasses, and she wears sensible stuff from L. L. Bean. She's very smart, but she's kind of slow at everything she does, because she has to really understand every single thing all the time. And once she understands it, she remembers everything. She remembers things that were in the newspaper when she was four. She remembers how much stamps used to cost before they cost whatever it is they cost now, which nobody but she knows either. Molly is two days younger than me, but sometimes I feel like she's about forty years older.

Molly doesn't mind being slow and sensible, but it sometimes drives other people crazy, especially Lisa, who just jumps into things. They make sort of a good pair, though, because Lisa is always dragging Molly into things, except when Molly is holding Lisa back from getting into who-knows-what kind of trouble. Me, I'm usually right in the middle, worrying about what will happen if we jump in too soon or hang back too long.

Lisa waved to me, I waved back, and the three of us converged on the first house on the block, the Ritters'. We rang the bell, full of enthusiasm. Nobody home.

We went to the second house. Just Mrs. Herbert, the baby-sitter, and Jesse, who was two. Nobody was going to buy magazines there.

The third house was mine. I had already gotten my dad to buy a subscription to *Country Roads.* I knew he'd never read it.

Luckily, it was a gorgeous day, the first of April, with a warm, damp wind blowing us down the street. The last little patches of dirty snow were melting fast, and tiny bright-green crocus shoots were pushing up right through the snow. Dormouth is a seacoast city, and our neighborhood is only a few blocks from the water; the smell of the ocean was really strong that day. All in all, it wasn't a bad day to be trudging around the neighborhood.

"Should we try starting a couple of blocks down, across the street?" Lisa asked.

I looked across the street, way down toward the traffic light at Cranberry Street, to see what the first house was.

Uh-oh.

It was Miss Hanson's house.

I gulped hard. Could I really ring Miss Hanson's doorbell? *Oh, come on,* I thought to myself. *Don't be such a chicken.* But it didn't help much.

Miss Hanson was my old piano teacher. She was a really good piano teacher and everything, but she didn't fool around. She was really strict. She expected dedication. She expected excellence. She expected no messed-up scales, no slumping at the keyboard, no lateness to lessons, no excuses about missed practicing.

She was just as tough on herself as on her students. She must have been way over 60, but she still shoveled her own snow, and got up on her roof to fix it. She wasn't married, and never had been: "Never saw the use in a husband," she had once told me.

Miss Hanson still rides her bicycle all around town, still stands straight as a broom, still thinks the president is a fool, the same thing she has thought of every other president.

Naturally, I was terrified of Miss Hanson, even though I knew she was sort of a neat person. When I was around her, I was always afraid I was doing something wrong, or was just about to. And two years ago, when I'd decided that I wanted to switch to the tuba instead of the piano, so I could play in the school band, I was a wreck for six months. I had finally given my fearless older brother, Pete, a dollar to go over to Miss Hanson's and tell her I was quitting. "It's never going to work," he'd said, pocketing the dollar.

Of course it didn't work. She told him I could quit but that I had to come and tell her myself. As I walked over there, my legs were shaking so hard I could hardly walk. But when I got there, an amazing thing happened.

She sat me down in her living room, gave me a cup of chamomile tea, and told me that it was my life and I shouldn't let anybody else live it for me. "If you want to play the tuba, then play the tuba. Where do you think I'd be today if I let people tell me what to do?" she said. She returned my piano music to me, patted me on the head, and told me she was sure I'd be a perfectly adequate tubist. I walked out the door in a daze.

And now I was going back to Miss Hanson's house.

Miss Hanson's Roommate

"Um, I think I hear my mother calling me," I said, doing an about-face on Miss Hanson's neat front walk.

"Don't be such a chicken," said Lisa.

"I'm sure she's not going to *eat* you," Molly said.

"She probably won't even remember you," said Lisa.

My mouth was dry as I marched up to the doorbell. Miss Hanson would remember me, all right. I could not manage to shake the two-year-old fear of getting yelled at. Nobody can inspire quite the same fear that a music teacher can.

She answered the door in a few seconds.

"Why, Eliza Spain!" she said. "What an unexpected pleasure!" Her frizzy hair stood around her head like a white lollipop, and her lively gray eyes looked me up and down.

She has high cheekbones, a straight nose, and a face that's lined and weatherbeaten from years of riding her bike in every season. It's a smart face. And since she smiles only when she feels like it, her smile is never faked. It's a nice smile. At this moment, I was very relieved to see it.

"Decided to give up the tuba and go back to the piano?" she said in that dry way she had. It had taken me about two years to be able to figure out when she was kidding around.

"Well, not exactly, Miss Hanson," I mumbled.

"I didn't think so," she said. "What can I do for you?"

"These are my friends Lisa and Molly," I said.

"Hello, Miss Hanson," Lisa and Molly sang.

"We're, um, trying to raise money?" I faltered.

"We're selling magazine subscriptions—" Lisa explained.

"For our fifth-grade trip," I said.

"To New York," Molly added.

"But you don't have to buy any if you don't want to," I said in a rush. "Really, it's okay."

"Perhaps you girls had better brush up your sales pitch a bit," said Miss Hanson with a laugh. "It's not too professional."

We all blushed at once.

"Well, come on in," said Miss Hanson. "Don't stand out there, for heaven's sake."

She held the door open and the three of us filed in. Her house was just as I remembered it.

Everything in Miss Hanson's house is simple, clean, and beautiful. There is no clutter anywhere. She doesn't have that much furniture, but what she has is carefully chosen. It's all made of beautiful wood. Lace curtains hang at the windows. Her wood floors gleam in the light that streams through the windows. I have always liked her house so much; it's the exact opposite of mine, which is completely jammed, every inch, with stuff: mail, homework, books, long-dead flowers, newspapers, chewed-up dog toys, magazines, shoes, bicycle wheels, you name it. Plus, Big has this long, silky red fur, and he sheds so much that the house is full of big balls of it. They look like tumbleweed. My mom is so busy with her veterinary practice, and my dad with his construction business, they don't have much time to spend cleaning up. And Pete and I just don't seem to have the tidiness gene. But that doesn't mean I don't find it really soothing to be in a house that's totally simple and calm, like Miss Hanson's.

Except—as I walked through Miss Hanson's familiar living room toward the kitchen—I noticed that things were not quite as perfect as they used to be. There were deep, messy scratches in the legs of the piano bench. The big braided rug under the grand piano was all frayed around the edges. And two of the lace curtains were shredded at the bottom. What on earth was going on here?

Miss Hanson never missed a thing, and she saw where my eyes were traveling. She smiled.

"Come into the kitchen, girls, and I'll make you some chamomile tea while you show me your magazines. And I'll introduce you to a friend of mine."

"Oh, gee, Miss Hanson, I didn't know you had company. We can come back another time, when we're not interrupting you," I apologized.

She smiled again. "Not at all. It's no interruption at all, trust me." She turned away slightly and coughed.

We trooped into the kitchen and sat down at the big round oak table. Molly took the magazine brochures out of her backpack and began spreading them out. One of them was so long, it dangled over the edge of the table and down toward the floor. I looked around for Miss Hanson's friend.

There was a small banging sound. *Whack*, it went. *Whack-whack.* It seemed to be coming from the floor. We looked down.

A black kitten with white boots and a white face was reaching up and batting at the dangling brochure.

"Oh, my gosh!" I cried. "It's a kitten!"

"Certainly is," said Miss Hanson, who was leaning against the kitchen doorway with her arms folded.

"Oh, he's so cute!" Lisa said. She jumped out of her chair and bent down to pet him, but he wasn't interested. He wanted to play with the paper.

"Look at him! He's adorable!" said Molly. "He looks just like Michele Geisler's kitten, the one she got the day you got poison ivy at the quarry last July." That was Molly and her memory.

Molly rustled the paper, and the kitten became so involved in batting it that he jumped too high, got off-balance, and landed on his back. He scrambled to his feet and started batting furiously at the paper again, until his claws caught in the paper and there was a loud *r-r-rip.*

"He and I will be great friends if I don't kill him first," said Miss Hanson.

"It's okay, I can tape the paper back together," said Molly.

"So *that's* what happened to your living room," I said to Miss Hanson.

"And my bedroom and my library," she added.

"What's his name?" Lisa asked. Now that Molly had folded up the brochure, the kitten was willing to let her pick him up. She nuzzled his belly with her nose. "He smells so good."

"His name is Sebastian," Miss Hanson replied. "Short for Johann Sebastian."

"As in Johann Sebastian Bach!" I said.

"Right you are, Eliza. I see that playing the tuba hasn't completely destroyed your memory."

Sebastian was now playing with a wisp of Lisa's hair. "Where did you get him, Miss Hanson?" she asked.

"I have a friend," Miss Hanson explained, "someone I play quartets with on Saturdays. Nettie Forster. She plays the cello. In her spare time, she volunteers at the animal shelter. One Saturday, just after New Year's, she told me about a kitten, a tiny little thing, which had been dumped at the door of the shelter the night before. Do you remember that big southwester we had just after Christmas?"

How could we forget it? It had been the nastiest storm of the winter, dumping ice, sleet, and snow for almost two solid days. One of the school buses had almost skidded off the road.

"Well, this kitten, its eyes barely open, had been left there on the doorstep at the height of the storm. It was tucked into a big red woolen Christmas stocking. Thank goodness it was crying and crying, or otherwise they might not have even noticed it when they locked up for the night. Nettie was very upset about this little fellow. Obviously, somebody had gotten him for Christmas, and then decided they didn't want him."

"Oh, that's *horrible!*" said Lisa.

"Happens a lot, apparently. Nettie tells me the animal shelter's biggest season is after the holidays. People give each other animals for presents without really thinking about whether it's a good idea."

"I know," I said. "My mother is always getting animals dumped on her after Christmas, too."

"So, before I knew it," continued Miss Hanson, "the words were out of my mouth. 'I'll adopt him,' I said. Little did I know he was the devil incarnate."

Sebastian, now blinking sleepily on Lisa's shoulder, looked like a little angel.

"He managed to get himself stuck in my clothes closet the other day," said Miss Hanson, shaking her head with a rueful smile. "By the time I heard him mewing and rescued him, he had shredded my best silk kimono, the one I got in Japan." She stopped and began coughing again, and this time she had trouble stopping.

"That doesn't sound like such a good cough, Miss Hanson," said Molly.

"No, it's fine. Just a pesky little thing I can't seem to shake. It's left over from a cold I had in the winter." She wiped the tears from her eyes with her sleeve.

Molly took Sebastian from Lisa and cradled him in her arms. I could hear him purring from several feet away.

"I brought him home from the shelter right in the red woolen stocking he was delivered in. He seemed to like it."

"I didn't know we had an animal shelter in Dormouth," said Lisa.

"Yes, it opened in 1978," said Molly.

We all just stared at her in amazement.

"I read it in the Sunday section of the newspaper," she explained, a little embarrassed.

"Well, the shelter may not be here for much longer," said Miss Hanson. "It may have to close. Lack of funds, like everything else these days."

"That's terrible," said Lisa.

"Yes, it is," said Miss Hanson. "But, unfortunately, that's life. Now, why don't I take a look at your magazines."

Miss Hanson made us all cups of lovely, mild chamomile tea, and we all sat down at the table. Miss Hanson is not one to agonize over a decision. She scanned the brochure quickly, and then said, "I'll take *Home Handyman*."

"Would you like it for twelve or twenty-four months?" asked Molly, all business. She had her pencil ready to fill out the form.

"Twelve," said Miss Hanson firmly. "I'm sure there's not much in there that I don't know." She gave a small snort. "'Home Handy*man*,' indeed."

"Thank you very much for your order," said Molly, folding up the papers. "You don't have to pay till you get your first issue."

"And thank you for inviting us in, and for the tea," said Lisa.

"And for introducing us to Sebastian," I added. "If you ever need me to take care of him or anything, please just call me. I'm good at taking care of animals. My mother's a vet, you know."

"I know," she replied. "She gave Sebastian his shots."

"We'll *all* help take care of him," said Lisa. "Any time you need help. He's *soooo* cute!"

"We'd love to cat-sit," said Molly.

Did I mention yet that Lisa and Molly are as crazy about animals as I am?

"Well, I'll certainly keep that in mind," said Miss Hanson.

She walked us to the door, and Sebastian rubbed himself around her ankles as we said goodbye.

"I suppose you three will be going to Mrs. Gresham's house next," said Miss Hanson. Her expression was hard to read.

But the three of us froze in our tracks.

"*Aaak!* I forgot Mrs. Gresham lives next door!" Lisa said.

"I think I hear my mother calling me," I said.

Our New Cause

Everybody in the whole neighborhood knows Mrs. Gresham. But nobody—from the littlest kid to the most imposing bank president—wants to deal with her. Because Mrs. Gresham is mean.

For some reason, everybody in Dormouth seems to know that Mrs. Gresham's husband ran off with a waitress about twenty years ago. Even the children know this. Everyone even knows that the waitress's name was Lillian, and that she had a squint.

After twenty years, Mrs. Gresham is still in a really, really bad mood about this. By all accounts, Mr. Gresham wasn't even a nice guy. But that doesn't seem to matter to Mrs. Gresham. I don't know what she was like before the day Mr. Gresham and Lillian took off for Miami. But Mrs. Gresham is now the bitterest, nastiest, sour-temperedest person you would ever hope not to meet. The rumor is that every day Mrs. Gresham runs to her mailbox, looking for the letter in which Mr. Gresham begs her to let him come crawling back to her. Then she'll refuse, and laugh in his face: Ha, ha, ha. But of course the letter never comes.

When we were halfway over to her house, Molly stopped. "Does it make any sense to even try selling her any magazines?" she asked.

"What's the worst that can happen?" said Lisa. "So she yells at us. What do we care? Maybe she'll even buy some magazines. She must read *something*."

"Yeah, *Meanie Monthly*," I said. "I don't think we carry that, do we?"

"Nope," said Molly glumly.

"Let's just try it. We can always run if she gets dangerous," said Lisa.

Hesitantly, we walked the rest of the way up the path to Mrs. Gresham's house. I felt like we were Hansel and Gretel knocking on the wicked witch's door. Lisa rang the bell.

The door was instantly yanked open; she must have been watching us from the window.

"What?" she demanded.

I could smell her perfume from outside. She wears frilly, lacy dresses and plenty of mascara and rouge. She seems to think she's a real cutie-pie. Her little mouth was twisted into a scowl.

Lisa, always the brave one, just jumped right in and started talking. "Hi," she said brightly. "We're selling magazine subscriptions to help pay for our school trip, and we wondered if you'd—"

"Forget it," Mrs. Gresham snapped. "I pay my taxes. That's as much support as I'm required to give you and your sorry excuse for a school. All they do is teach you all to be little hoodlums anyway. I'll bet the three of you are carrying machine guns. Now, I'll thank you to stop disturbing my peace or I'll call the police." She closed the door with a bang.

Molly sighed. "We tried," she said.

I wasn't used to being treated like that. I was practically shaking as we walked down her path. Never, never, as long as I lived, I vowed to myself, would I go near that woman again.

Her door flew open. "And don't trample on the rosebushes!" she shouted.

Oh, yes. Mrs. Gresham's famous rosebushes. She's always winning prizes with them. It's a wonder that everything she touches doesn't wither and die, but she does seem to have the knack of growing great roses. Either that or the judges are scared not to give her the awards. Anyhow, Mrs. Gresham is out there in her yard all spring and summer, in her mascara and lipstick, fussing like a maniac with her rosebushes. Anybody who so much as breathes on them is taking their life in their hands.

"How can Miss Hanson stand to live next door to her?" Lisa wondered aloud as we walked down the sidewalk, being *very* careful not to go near the rosebushes.

"I don't think they like each other very much at all," I said. "In the warm weather, during my lessons, Mrs. Gresham was always yelling through the windows at Miss Hanson to stop making so much noise. And one time, when Miss Hanson was playing Beethoven with her friends, Mrs. Gresham actually called the police! Miss Hanson lost it that time. She told Mrs. Gresham she was a rotten old hag, and said she should go stick her head in a bucket. She told me about it later."

"Wow!" said Lisa admiringly.

"As you can imagine, their relationship didn't get any better after that incident," I said. "Mrs. Gresham keeps calling the cops on Miss Hanson, but they never even bother coming. They know Mrs. Gresham is out of her mind."

We were now in front of the next house on the block. "Should we try this one?" Lisa asked.

"This is Abby Goodman's house, I think," I said. "There probably won't be anybody home."

"You're right," said Lisa. "I guess we might as well try it, though." We walked up to the yellow front door.

We all knew why there wasn't likely to be anybody home. Abby is not the kind of person who hangs around her house after school. She's much too busy. She has things to do.

Abby Goodman is one of those people whose life looks more perfect than yours could ever be. First of all, she looks perfect. She has strawberry blond hair that just leaps into any style she wants. Of course, she always puts it in a ponytail when she's doing gymnastics. And this is not just cute little school gymnastics—this is national meets, which she sometimes wins. She just moved to Dormouth in the middle of last year, because there's a good coach here. She also rides horses in a serious way and, oh, yes, she does a little modeling work when she has the time. And she has incredible clothes, because sometimes they give her the clothing from the ads. Abby is in the same grade as us. She gets A's.

Naturally, we hated her.

Well, we didn't, technically, hate *her,* because we didn't know her well enough to hate her. We just sort of hated the *idea* of her. We hated her on principle.

We rang the bell, but nobody was home, as we expected. Abby lives with her father, and he's always taking her to her meets and practices and jobs and everything else. Nobody knew exactly where her mother was.

After Abby's house, we went to four more houses, and we sold a total of one more subscription: a year of *Beautiful Home* to the Albertson family, whose house looked about ten times worse than mine.

"I'm ready to stop," I said when we were back to my house. "I really have to go home and practice my tuba. And I have three pages of math homework to do, too."

"Okay," said Molly. "But we only made $5.64 for the class trip today. Let's see...today's Monday. Do you want to go out again tomorrow or Wednesday?"

"Tomorrow is good for me," said Lisa. "Wednesday I have art class. But, listen, I had this idea."

"Yeah?" I said, worrying about my homework. "Is it a fast idea?"

"Yes. Here it is. I've been wondering about something Miss Hanson said. Maybe we could raise money for the animal shelter, so it doesn't need to close."

"Oh, Lisa, I don't know, I don't have time. I've got homework and practicing and selling magazines—" I started whining.

"If the animal shelter closes, there won't be any place for stray dogs and cats to go, and they'll all get hit by cars or die in the winter. We *have* to help. It's even more important than the class trip."

"What could *we* do to raise money? We don't have any magazines to sell. We're just kids," I said, still whining.

"I have an idea," said Molly. "We could bake cookies and brownies. Remember what good brownies you and I baked last year for your Aunt Ella's birthday? September 29, remember?"

"Yeah, I remember. They were good," I conceded. Even *I* didn't know my aunt's birthday without looking at the calendar.

Molly was really getting into the idea. "And maybe if we raise money, and get some publicity for our helping the animal shelter, other people will start helping too," she said.

"Great idea," said Lisa. "When can we start baking?"

"How about Friday?" Molly suggested.

"How about Thursday?" I said, giving up. "Then we can sell the cookies on Friday."

"Okay," said Lisa. "Thursday."

"Thursday," I said.

Celebrities

I got to Lisa's house first on Thursday.

I love going to Lisa's. She has this whole big extended family. Some of them live there and some just visit a lot, but the list of who's who keeps changing. There are always a lot of aunts and uncles and cousins there. Lisa and her parents live there all the time, of course, and also her grandmother, who I love to pieces. She's a tiny old lady who speaks almost no English, but she and I always communicate just fine. She likes to braid my hair the way she braids Lisa's, chuckling the whole time over its impossibleness. I always try to remember to bring her peppermint candies, because she likes them so much.

Lisa's parents are both doctors, and they do Western and Eastern medicine in their clinic. Lisa's mother once offered to try acupuncture on me to help heal a sprained ankle I had. It was nice of her to offer, but I just couldn't handle the idea of those needles. Ugh.

When I got to Lisa's, Lisa was already setting everything up in the kitchen. "We can't make a big mess like we did that time we made dinner," she said to me. "My parents were not happy. Even when dinner turned out edible, they were not happy."

"I guess it was the mashed potatoes on the ceiling," I said ruefully.

"Among other things," said Lisa. "So let's try to keep the brownie batter in the bowl this time."

Molly arrived, and the three of us got to work, being a lot less silly than we'd been the time we'd made dinner. After all, this was serious business. This was saving the animal shelter.

When we were done, we had four batches of brownies and six batches of oatmeal cookies.

"Whew," I said, wiping my sweaty brow. "That's hard work."

"To say nothing of the weight-gain problem," said Lisa, munching on a warm oatmeal cookie. "After all, we have to test them to make sure they're good."

"We have to test a lot of them," I agreed, taking two.

We put them away before we could test any more.

The next morning, I stopped by Lisa's house. We put six shoeboxes full of cookies and brownies into Lisa's old red wagon, and pulled it to school.

After school, we borrowed a little table from the science room and set it up in the lobby. COOKIES FOR A CAUSE, our sign said. 15¢ EACH.

Molly came running over when we were almost done setting up. "I stayed a little late to talk to Mr. Seligman about why you can't divide anything by zero," she explained, panting. "I just needed to *understand* it." Lisa rolled her eyes.

Molly looked anxiously down the hallway to the front door of the school. "They didn't show up yet?" she asked us.

"Who?" Lisa asked, straightening the sign.

"The people from Channel 7 News," Molly replied. "I called them up the other day, and they said they thought it was a nice story and they'd probably come over after school today to film us."

"Cool!" said Lisa.

"That's great, Molly!" I said. "I hope they come."

Molly looked nervously at her watch.

"Maybe they had a better story to cover," said Lisa. "Maybe there's a big disaster someplace."

"I hope not," said Molly, her eyes on the door.

Kids started noticing our sign, and the cookies began going fast. Everybody thought saving the animal shelter was a great idea. Plus, it being 3:15, everybody was hungry. Even the teachers bought some. The principal bought a whole box—she was going to a friend's house for dinner.

"Hey! Look!" Molly cried. "They came!" Sure enough, walking down the hall toward us was a woman with a large video camera on her shoulder and a man in a suit.

"It's James Johnson!" Lisa whooped. "I see him on TV all the time!"

The two of them approached us. "Are you the young ladies who are trying to save the animal shelter?" James Johnson asked us.

"Yes, we are," answered Lisa, the natural spokesgirl of our group, being the least shy by a long shot.

"Very nice sign," he said, reading it. "Make sure you get the sign, Andi," he said to the camerawoman. She pointed the camera at the sign and turned it on.

"Wait, wait, wait!" Lisa interjected. "Don't start shooting yet! We all look awful!" We all took a second to brush our hair madly and straighten our clothes.

"Okay," said Lisa.

He started interviewing us. "So you girls are trying to save the animal shelter," he said.

"Yes," Lisa said. "We heard it might have to close because there wasn't enough money, so we're trying to help."

"And we think it would be nice if other people tried to help too," said Molly, leaning toward the camera.

"What are your names?" he asked us. I noticed with embarrassment that when I said mine, my voice was shaking. I was really nervous.

Everybody who came over to buy cookies stuck their faces in the camera and waved.

The reporter asked us some more questions, and then got ready to wind it up. "Does the animal shelter know about you doing this?" he asked.

We looked at each other. "Um...not yet," said Lisa. "We sort of never thought of telling them."

James Johnson and the camerawoman

laughed. "Well, they will now," he said.

In another ten minutes, the two of them had packed up and were gone. Molly, Lisa, and I could not stop talking. Kids were milling around us, too. We were celebrities. For a minute, anyhow.

"Do you think it went well?" Molly asked.

Lisa and I bobbed our heads. "Yes. Definitely."

We went over every answer we had given and agreed that they had all been stupid.

Finally, half an hour later, all the cookies and brownies were gone, and we were calming down.

"I wonder how much we made," said Lisa as she packed up the sign and the boxes.

Molly counted the money and stuffed it into the envelope she had of course remembered to bring. "Thirty-one dollars and seventy-five cents," she said.

"Great!" I said.

"Let me make sure that's right," said Molly. "We had 120 cookies and 100 brownies. That's 220. I counted them yesterday. Okay: 220 times 15 is thirty-three dollars. Oh, no, we're a dollar twenty-five short!" She started counting the money again in a panic.

"Molly, stop worrying about it!" Lisa yelped. "It's close enough! We probably ate the extras! Don't be such a fussbudget!"

"I just think it's important to have accurate information," said Molly, slightly hurt.

"It's okay, Molly," I said, feeling a little bad for her. I always find myself protecting her. I understand her really well. We've never had one fight in our lives, which is more than I can say for anybody else I know. But her nit-pickiness does sometimes have a tendency to drive other people up a wall, even people who like her, like Lisa.

"So," said Lisa, "I guess we better go give this money to the animal shelter."

"Yeah," I agreed. "They don't even know we exist yet."

"Could we go now?" said Lisa.

"I can't," I said. "I promised my mom I'd stop by her office on my way home and help her clean the cages."

"Oh, the glamorous veterinarian business," said Lisa. She knew exactly how glamorous it was, because she had helped me clean out the cages a couple of times.

"Well," said Molly, "how about tomorrow?"

Lisa and I nodded.

"About eleven?" said Lisa. Molly and I agreed.

I really had to go. I had promised my

mother I'd be at her office at five, and it was almost five now. Plus, I had to run home first and walk Big, Little, and Archie.

When I got home, the three of them went nuts as soon as I walked in the door. I grabbed the three leashes from the nail inside the coat-closet door. "You wanna go for a walk?" I asked them. Of course, they got about ten times more nuts when I said the actual words. Little almost got trampled in the excitement.

I gave them a really fast walk, hurrying them along to the big empty lot where I always took them. Then I turned them around and marched them home.

"Sorry, guys, I gotta go," I said, closing the door in their disappointed faces. "I'll be home soon. Talk amongst yourselves."

At twenty-three minutes after five, I burst into my mom's office, which is actually a separate wing at the side of our big old ramshackle Victorian house. As I was hanging my jacket on a hook on the wall, I heard someone call my name. I turned around and found myself face to face with Abby Goodman.

Abby

"Abby!" I said. "What are you doing here? I mean—do you have a pet?" I never would have thought she was the pet type.

"No," she said. "I really love animals, but my father's never let me have one. I'm too busy. I'm hoping maybe now—"

My mother came out of her examination room. "Hi, Eliza," she said. "Hi, Abby." She sat down next to Abby and looked at a large cardboard box that I hadn't noticed at Abby's feet. "I'm glad you called me. Let's see your little friend." She opened the box carefully, and I crowded in to see what was in the box.

It was a baby raccoon! It was as cute as anything. But because I was my mother's daughter, I knew all the words in the lecture that was about to hit Abby.

My mother sighed. "Abby," she said, "where did you get this little guy?"

"He was all huddled up next to our garage door when my dad and I got home from practice today. I just had to save him. I'm naming him Bandit because of his mask."

My mother sighed again. "This raccoon is really adorable, Abby. I know you meant well, but you probably didn't do him any favors by picking him up. First of all, his mother probably hung around for a while, out of sight, until you took him. Second of all, it could have been dangerous for you. There's a lot of rabies around, and you never know with raccoons. Please, promise me you will never pick up a wild animal baby again."

"I promise," said Abby, looking really sad. "So then I can't keep him?"

"No, you can't," said my mother. "You have to know a lot to take care of a wild animal. It's not like having a pet." She took a pad and pen out of the pocket of her white coat. "Luckily, I know a woman who takes care of wild animals until they're old enough to be let go. Here's her number. Call her, and I'm sure she'll take this little fellow." She handed the phone number to Abby.

"Thank you," said Abby. Her chin was trembling.

"There's no charge for this visit," said my mother.

The phone rang in the back room. "Gotta get it," said my mom. "Eloise is sick today, and I'm going a little nuts. Come on in the back when you're ready, sweetie," she said to me.

After my mother was gone, Abby just sat there staring down into the box. A tear ran down her cheek. I was really surprised that this little raccoon would mean so much to her.

"I just fell so in love with him," she said. "I wanted to take care of him."

"It's too bad," I said. "Maybe you could get a puppy or something instead."

"No," she said sadly. "I really can't have any pets. My dad probably wouldn't even have let me keep this raccoon. I'm always having to practice, having to go to meets, having to do modeling jobs—" Her chin was trembling.

With a jolt, I realized that there was a whole other side to being Abby Goodman, and that her life wasn't as perfect as it seemed. She had a lot of pressure on her. No wonder she wanted to have a cute little raccoon to take care of and love.

I had a sudden impulse. "Abby," I said, "a couple of us—Lisa and Molly and I—are raising money to help save the animal shelter.

We're going over there tomorrow. Do you want to come? Maybe you could help us raise some more money, too."

Abby's eyes filled up with tears all over again. "Could I really?" She looked so grateful, I was almost embarrassed. "Nobody really ever asks me to do anything," she said. "I guess everybody thinks I'm too busy, or stuck-up, or something."

"I never thought you were stuck-up," I said, not entirely truthfully. "But I did think you were too busy."

"Thanks for asking me. I can go, because I hurt my knee and I can't work out tomorrow. Should I come over here?"

"Sure, that would be fine. Eleven o'clock."

"Great!" She stood up. "I'd better go home and call this lady about the raccoon," she said.

"Okay," I said. "See you."

I could see that she was walking with a slight limp. She waved as she closed the door.

I went in the back and rolled up my sleeves. "Thanks for helping today, Eliza," said my mother as I started changing newspaper in the cages. "I get so frazzled when Eloise isn't here, sometimes I just can't think straight. And I had a Saint Bernard having a litter today, on top of everything else. She had a hard time. I had to give her a lot of help." She pointed her chin toward the corner. There, on a big pillow, was the enormous dog, looking very, very tired. There were three little puppies in a pile next to her. "That's Topsy," said my mom.

"Hi, Topsy," I said. Topsy didn't even open her eyes.

My mother had to keep answering the phone as I went around the room cleaning the cages and petting sick dogs and cats. "Don't touch that chow," my mother called, covering the receiver with her hand. "He feels crummy. He might bite you."

"Okay," I said, giving him a wide berth.

As I worked, I started thinking about Abby, and I was feeling good about asking her along. She really seemed like a nice person after all. Who would have thought a person like her was lonely? Lisa and Molly would like her when they got to know her, I was sure....

Or would they? Suddenly my good mood started to turn icky. I was sure Molly would be okay about Abby, but Lisa might be another story. She has very definite likes and dislikes. One of our biggest fights had been in the third grade, when she'd decided she hated our friend Amanda, and she hadn't been able to stand it that I still wanted to stay friends with Amanda. Lisa wanted me to hate Amanda, too, and she was so mad at me for still talking to her that she stopped talking to *me* for three days. That's how Lisa is.

I decided I'd better call her as soon as I got home.

And that's what I did. I told her the whole story of how I had run into Abby, and how she brought the baby raccoon to my mother's, and how nice she seemed to be, and how I had invited her along for tomorrow.

"This is just kind of a big huge surprise, Eliza. Abby the Extremely Perfect? And you asked her to come along? Without even telling us?"

"It was kind of a spur-of-the-moment thing," I said defensively. "But, Lisa, I think she might be really nice when you get to know her. Nobody ever asks her to do anything. Everybody always thinks she's so perfect they can't go near her. I'm sorry I asked her without asking you first, but there she was. I was swept away by the moment. Couldn't we give it a try? Please? I'll be your best friend."

This is a joke we have. It's a stupid thing left over from the playground when we were six. Plus, it's a joke because I basically *am* her best friend, anyway.

"Okay, okay," said Lisa. "I just think she's kind of unreliable. Last year she came into my class, and we had to work in groups on this project on the Pacific Ocean. She was supposed to make a diorama of the ocean floor for her part of it, and she was really late because she had to do an advertisement for toothpaste or something, and all of us got a grade lower. So I hope she actually turns up tomorrow. I'm not waiting around all day for her."

"This means a lot to her," I said.

"All right," said Lisa. "I trust your judgment....I think."

"You won't be sorry," I said. "She's nice. You'll see."

When I hung up the phone, my mother came in the door. "Whew, what a day," she said, falling onto the sofa and kicking off her shoes. She winced at the sound of Pete practicing his drums upstairs. "I hate it when Eloise isn't there. Thanks for helping me out."

The phone rang once, then it stopped. Pete must have picked it up upstairs. "Eliza, it's for you!" he called down the stairs.

"Who is it?" I yelled back.

I heard him running down the stairs, and

his head poked around the landing. He cupped his hands over his mouth so I'd be able to hear him whisper. "It's Miss Hanson!"

Sebastian Looks for Trouble

"Hello?" I said, hardly believing it. Miss Hanson hadn't ever called me, even when she was my teacher.

"Hello, Eliza," she said. Her voice sounded a little strange, a little shaky.

"Hi, Miss Hanson, how are you?" I said.

"Actually, dear, I'm not too well. I'm calling you from the hospital. I seem to have come down with a case of walking pneumonia. The doctor says I've probably had it for weeks, but I just didn't pay it any mind. Now I'm stuck here for at least a week."

"Oh, that's awful, Miss Hanson!" I said. "I hope you feel better soon."

"I'm sure I will. But my big problem is Sebastian. I thought I was just coming over here for an X-ray, but they checked me in. Sebastian is all alone, with not much food and only a little water. Could I take you up on

43

your kind offer of help with him?"

"Of course!" I said. "Should I bring him back here to my house?"

"I think cats would rather stay in familiar surroundings than get used to someplace new. If you and your friends could stop by and feed and water him once or twice a day, maybe play with him for a little while, I think he'll be just fine. You can let him out if you keep an eye on him. And maybe you could also check to make sure he hasn't locked himself into a closet."

"Sure we can. But how can we get into your house?"

"That's easy," she said. "There's a key hidden under a loose brick at the edge of the walkway. It's the third brick from the end, on the left side. And the cat food is in the cabinet over the stove."

"Do you think I could go over there in the morning?" I asked.

"Sure. He's got enough food for today."

"Don't worry about a thing, Miss Hanson. My friends and I will take good care of Sebastian until you're better."

"That's a big worry off my mind," she said. "Now I'll be able to concentrate on getting rid of this ridiculous pneumonia."

She thanked me, and we said goodbye.

I immediately called Lisa. "Guess what?" I said breathlessly.

"The sky is falling?" she guessed.

"No, you twerp. Miss Hanson is in the hospital with pneumonia and we're going to take care of Sebastian for a week!"

"Great! I mean, terrible! I mean, I don't know what I mean. Great and terrible. Is she going to be okay?"

"I think so," I said. "She's pretty strong."

"Should Molly and I meet you over there in the morning?"

"Yeah, and I was thinking maybe Abby could meet us too. She lives right by there, remember."

"Okay, okay," said Lisa grudgingly.

I figured that since I had called Lisa to tell her about Abby, maybe I should call Molly too. I didn't think she'd have any problem, but it seemed fair. I dialed her number and told her what the story was.

"Okay," she said. That was it.

"So, um, I'll see you in the morning?"

"Yup. Bye," said Molly. She was not one for long, aimless phone conversations like the ones I had with most of my other friends. She didn't see the point.

A second later, the phone rang. "I forgot to tell you," said Molly. "They called me

45

from the TV station. They're showing the story about us on the 10 o'clock news tonight!"

"Wow!" I said. It was kind of a complicated "wow" though. It meant, "Wow! Great!" and also, "Wow! I'm about to die of embarrassment and never be able to show my face in school again!"

At 9:59 I was sitting rigidly on the sofa, waiting for the news to start. My whole family was on the sofa with me. Little was curled up in my lap, and Archie was slung across Pete's lap. Big couldn't fit, so he lay on the floor on my mother's feet.

By the time we'd sat through twenty minutes of fires, robberies, and wars, we were pretty numb. But then, at 10:21, after the commercial, there we were—Lisa, Molly, and me. We could see why they wanted to run a story like ours on the news: we were a nice break from all the bad news, just a sweet little story about girls and an animal shelter.

All my worst fears were confirmed: I looked amazingly horrible. My hair was frizzed out all over the place, and my glasses looked like bug eyes.

"Nice look, Eliza," said Pete.

"Shut up," I said.

"Be nice, Pete," said my mother. "It's very hard to look at yourself on TV."

"Especially when you look like the Bride of Frankenstein," said Pete, drumming on Archie's belly.

"More like the Sister of Frankenstein," I retorted, unable as usual to think of anything but a no-brain comeback.

"Shhh," said my father. "I want to hear."

It was over in about thirty seconds, to my great relief. They had hardly used anything we'd said, but they had used the part where Molly told other people to help.

"Great work," said my dad. "You guys should be proud of yourselves." My mother hugged me. Even Pete drummed on my head to show his approval.

The next morning at ten, we all met in front of Miss Hanson's house. The plan was that we'd play with Sebastian for a while and then go to the animal shelter. While I was waiting for the others, I caught a glimpse of Mrs. Gresham looking at me from behind the curtain of her upstairs window; when I looked at her, she dropped the curtain.

Molly and Lisa got there at the same time.

"Did you *see* us?" shrieked Lisa.

"It was kind of like watching an accident,"

I said. "I wanted to look away, but I couldn't."

"I think we were great," said Molly.

"I saw you," said Abby, running down the street toward us. "My dad was watching, and he called me in. You *were* great!"

"Oh, hi, Abby," said Lisa. "You thought we looked okay?"

"You all looked totally cool," she assured us. "I felt proud to be your friend."

Lisa looked genuinely surprised. "That's so nice," she said.

"Let's see if people give the shelter any money," said Molly.

I looked under the brick for the key. It was right where it was supposed to be, and it worked easily in the lock. And when we got inside, Sebastian was *so* happy to see us. He rubbed in and out of our ankles, and then immediately started attacking the long fringe that hung from Lisa's suede jacket.

"He's so cute!" Abby said.

"Mr. Personality," I said, looking for the cat food over the stove. It was right there, three boxes neatly lined up. This would definitely last until Miss Hanson got home.

"Eliza," said Lisa, "I feel kind of bad for Sebastian. He's cooped up in here all alone. Do you think maybe we could let him play outside for a little while?"

"Well," I said, pouring some food into his little bowl, "Miss Hanson did say we could let him out if we kept an eye on him. I don't know, though—it makes me kind of nervous…"

"We'll be really careful," Abby said. "Why don't we all go outside?"

"That's a good idea," said Lisa. "We could sit on the ground in a circle and make him stay inside the circle."

I kind of doubted that we could make him stay anywhere, but I decided to go along with it. Poor little Sebastian, all cooped up inside.

We took him out into the backyard. Molly carried him. It was a beautiful day, bright, warm, and sunny, and the snow was now all melted away. The four of us sat down on the brown grass, and Molly put Sebastian in the center of the circle.

"Sebastian! *Psss-psss,*" said Lisa, trying to get his attention with a rubber band she had in her pocket. He went over to her and started playing with it, rolling over onto his back from joy and silliness. I began to relax. We were doing fine.

Suddenly, he stopped playing with the rubber band and froze, staring as if he had noticed something in the distance. And then, quick as a shot, he bolted, too fast for us to stop him. He streaked straight over toward Mrs. Gresham's yard, at about a hundred miles an hour. Abby made a flying leap for him—it was actually very impressive, gymnastically speaking—but he was gone. We all jumped up and ran after him, but Sebastian knew exactly what he wanted to do: make trouble. He was making a beeline for a tiny, young, tender rosebush in Mrs. Gresham's yard. It was all tied up with red string to hold it onto a wooden stake. The string had some kind of gold threads in it, and glinted and fluttered in the sunlight. Of course, Sebastian was *very* interested in the string.

He was way ahead of us. He started poking at the string, looking to see if it was any fun. He saw that if he poked it hard, the bush moved. So he poked it harder, until his claw was caught in it. That made him mad, and he pushed at it with his other paw, which also got caught, so he got his back feet involved, trying to push himself away from the thing, and now he was completely tangled up in the string.

All of this happened in about fourteen seconds, and by the time we had caught up to him he was completely fouled up. He was fighting like a little tiger, and none of us could get hold of him. He had those tiny, sharp claws out, too.

Mrs. Gresham came bombing out of her house with a broom. She started whacking at Sebastian and screaming, "My best rosebush! My expensive rosebush from England! I'll kill him, the little criminal! Do you know how rare that rosebush is?"

Mrs. Gresham dropped the broom and clamped her gnarly hands around Sebastian's neck and pulled him off the rosebush. Unfortunately, he was so tangled up that along with him came the string—and the rosebush, pulled out by the roots.

"Stop!" Lisa yelled. "You're choking him!"

By this time, Sebastian was totally freaked out. He looked wild. Mrs. Gresham looked wild too.

"Maybe I can help with him," Abby said. She began disentangling Sebastian, one paw at a time, from the rosebush. Her hands were getting scratched both from the thorns and from Sebastian's claws, but she kept going. Mrs. Gresham just stood there, looking as if she was going to blast off straight up, like the Space Shuttle.

"Oh, Mrs. Gresham, we're really sorry!" I said. "This is all our fault. We should never have let him out. It's just that Miss Hanson is in the hospital, and we're taking care of him, and we thought he'd stay in the yard, and—"

"Well, you thought wrong, didn't you, young lady?" She didn't even pretend to be concerned about Miss Hanson.

"We'll make it up to you, we promise," said Lisa. "We can replant the rosebush in a pot, and maybe it will live, or we'll pay for a new one—" She tried to take the rosebush.

"Don't touch that, you'll only kill it," snapped Mrs. Gresham. "And get out of my yard. You're trespassing. I'll have to decide whether to have you arrested. Take that cat with you. If I see it in my yard again, I swear I'm going to do something unpleasant to it. Now, get out of here."

"Yes, ma'am," I said. I had never called anybody "ma'am" in my life, but this situation seemed to call for it.

"We promise we won't let him out anymore," I said as we backed away.

"I'll say you won't." She clenched her fists. "I hate cats. Disgusting animals. Now get out of here before I call the police."

She turned on her heel and marched back to her house, slamming the door behind her.

We ran for Miss Hanson's house, and fell all over ourselves getting in the door. First we panted for a while, and then Lisa started giggling. One by one we all started giggling. We couldn't help it. It was probably nerves, or the release of all that tension.

"I'll get you, my pretty!" said Lisa in her meanest Wicked Witch of the West voice.

"And your little dog Toto, too!" cackled Abby.

We collapsed on the floor, laughing. Every time we were about to stop, somebody would start us off again.

Finally, we stopped laughing and picked ourselves up off the floor. We were all holding our stomachs. Sebastian was already curled up on a chair, looking bored, the little brat. He was clearly none the worse for wear.

"Well, I guess that's the last time we let Sebastian out," I said.

"Unless we get him a little leash," said Lisa.

"Yeah, right," I said.

Molly looked at the kitchen clock. "Maybe we should head over to the animal shelter," she said. "My mom is going to take me shopping this afternoon."

We hung around with Sebastian for a little longer, petting him and trying to get him interested in his cat food, and then we locked up the house. I glanced up at Mrs. Gresham's window just in time to see a slight rustling of the curtain. That woman gave me the creeps.

She obviously had nothing better to do than to spy out her windows all the time.

We walked downtown to the animal shelter. Molly and Abby walked about half a block ahead of me and Lisa. I was kicking a rock. At first it was no big deal, but after I still had the rock on the third block it became sort of a thing. I couldn't lose it.

"Do you like Abby better now?" I asked Lisa in a low voice.

"She's great! You just have to get to know her. She's not stuck-up at all. And she was so cool when she got Sebastian away from Mrs. Gresham."

"I'm glad you like her," I said.

I had to go up onto somebody's lawn to get my rock back. I kicked it onto the sidewalk.

"I was wondering," Lisa said. "Do you think Mrs. Gresham might ever really do something bad to Sebastian?"

My rock bounced into a storm drain.

"She better not," I muttered. "She just better not."

"Look," said Lisa. "There's the animal shelter." Abby and Molly were already going in.

The animal shelter was a noisy place. As soon as you passed the front desk you were in the adoption area. There were rows and rows of cages full of dogs, and more rows with cats.

Before we dropped off the money, we decided to take a look at the animals. All four of us started down the first aisle of dogs.

There were big ones and little ones, puppies and old, gray ones. Some wagged their tails when we got near their cages, and some just looked depressed. From hanging around my mother's office, I could tell a lot about their stories. Like, the ones that had really dull coats and torn-up pads on their paws had probably been out and running for a while. The ones that winced when you lifted your hand to pet them had been abused.

I couldn't help stopping at almost every cage to say hello. Some of the dogs would stand up and try to lick me through the wire mesh. A few of them had collars and even tags, but most of them, I could tell, were strays. There was one big, shaggy brown one with a folded-down ear that I fell totally in love with.

By the end of the first aisle I was a wreck. We all were. "I want to take all of them home!" Abby wailed.

"So do I!" I wailed back.

But we knew we couldn't. Some of them would get adopted, and some would not.

"How can people just dump their pets

when they get tired of taking care of them?" Lisa said angrily. "I can't understand how anybody could do that. It makes me so mad!"

I couldn't understand it any better than she could, and I was sure the people who ran the shelter couldn't either. They just had to deal with all the dogs and cats.

We went to the front desk. A pretty woman was there filling out some forms. "I'll be with you in just a second," she said, barely looking up.

"We were wondering if we could see the manager. I mean, the president. I mean, the person in charge," I said brilliantly.

She looked up. She looked from me to Lisa to Molly, as if she was trying to remember something about us. Then she did.

"You're the girls who were raising the money for us!" she exclaimed. She jumped up and ran toward an office across the lobby. The sign next to the door said DIRECTOR.

"Ms. Washington! It's the girls from the 10 o'clock news! They're here!"

A woman came out of the office and hurried toward us. "Why, so they are," she said, beaming. "We've been trying to find you girls. We called the television station, but they wouldn't release any information about you. Very right of them. But then we realized that sooner or later you'd be coming in with the money you raised. We hoped you would, anyway."

We all laughed. Molly pulled out the envelope with the money. "It's right here," she said, handing it over.

Ms. Washington looked into the envelope. "This is wonderful, just wonderful, girls," she said. She really looked moved. "And even more important than the money is the publicity you managed to get for us. Now people know that our shelter is in jeopardy."

"So it's really true?" Lisa said.

"It is indeed. We thought we might only last a few weeks more. Oh, there was a small article in the paper. Nobody took much notice. But people really paid attention to you girls. In fact, a man came by this morning and dropped off a check for five hundred dollars! He said he'd seen you on the news and he wanted to help. Other people have been calling, too."

"That's great!" said Molly.

After some more people who worked at the animal shelter came over to meet us and thank us, we headed home. We felt pretty darned good.

Killer Fudge

We weren't allowed to visit Miss Hanson in the hospital because we were kids, but I did talk to her a couple of times on the phone. She assured me that she was getting better, and I assured her that Sebastian was happy. We were going over there twice a day, either together or alone, and playing with him. We weren't letting him out anymore, though. I didn't tell Miss Hanson about the little incident with Mrs. Gresham. But she did happen to mention that she had let Sebastian out a few times, and he had always made straight for Mrs. Gresham's rosebushes. Miss Hanson seemed kind of pleased about it. "That Emily Gresham was really steamed," she said with satisfaction.

Miss Hanson was very interested to hear about how the four of us were raising money for the animal shelter. "Good for you," she said. I told her that we were planning to sell fudge in school on Friday, and she said that the doctor was saying he'd probably let her out on Friday.

"We'll come by after school and bring you some fudge," I said.

"That would be just lovely," she said.

I really liked not having Miss Hanson for a teacher anymore. It was a lot easier now that I didn't have to be terrified of her.

Lisa and I had decided to make fudge on Thursday, even though Molly and Abby both had things to do after school that day.

"Do you think we could go to your house to cook this time?" Lisa asked. "It might be good to take turns, so my family doesn't get tired of us taking over the kitchen."

"And besides," I said slyly, "Pete might be there."

Lisa blushed a deep red.

Lisa has the most gigantic crush on my big brother. Pete's thirteen. I think he's pretty much a doofus, but my parents keep telling me he'll be great when he's a grown-up.

The problem is that Pete doesn't know Lisa is alive. He doesn't know any girl is alive. This might partly be because he can't see them; his hair falls right into his eyes, and he's always having to sort of whip his head to the side so he can see where he's going. Lisa goes nuts when he does this. She thinks it's totally irresistible.

Pete plays the drums. He's in a band called the Screaming Mimis. They practice in his friend Max's garage. Pete practices every second he's awake, though. If he doesn't have drumsticks, he uses pencils, or spoons, or his hands. If he doesn't have drums he uses his thighs, or the top of the microwave, or my head (that's his favorite). He's always grunting these tuneless little tunes, that go like this: *Uh*, uh-uh *uh*, uh-uh *uh*-uh *uuuh*. He wants me to try playing rock tuba. He says I could be in the Screaming Mimis. Once, Pete wired my tuba up to Max's huge guitar amplifier. After he got the whole thing hooked up, I played an E flat. It blew out all the windows in Max's garage.

"Cool," Pete said.

On Thursday, Lisa came straight home from school with me. When we got to my house, we started setting up to make fudge. Pete was playing his drums upstairs.

"How can you stand to live with somebody so cool?" sighed Lisa.

"I can stand it," I said.

I got out the one cookbook my parents

have: *How to Make Anything in Under 20 Minutes.* As I said, my parents don't have much time to be domestic.

Lisa propped her elbows up on the counter and read aloud from the cookbook. Big, Little, and Archie had all gathered in the kitchen to see if any good stuff was coming their way. They were sitting at attention under the counter, arranged by size. Lisa scratched Big behind the ears as she read.

"Pot," she said.

"Check," I said, putting one on the stove.

"Sugar."

"Check," I said. "We're doing great here. What's next?" I heaved the bag onto the counter.

"Candy thermometer."

"No check," I said, rummaging in the kitchen-gadget drawer. "Nobody in this family has ever made candy in their lives."

"Okay, maybe we can sort of estimate. Let's see, what's next...unsweetened chocolate."

I looked in the closet. "No check."

"Uh-oh," said Lisa.

"Hold on a second. I have a Hershey bar in my jacket pocket. Think we could use that?"

She shrugged. "I dunno. Maybe."

I dug it out and put it on the counter. I

also found a can of chocolate syrup in the cabinet.

We had all the other ingredients, most of them very old packages in the back of the cabinet, except walnuts.

I rummaged around. "We have pumpkin seeds," I said. "What do you think?"

"I dunno," she said again.

I put the pumpkin seeds on the counter. "At least they'll be interesting," I said. "Who knows, maybe we're inventing a new classic recipe here. Hershey-bar-and-chocolate-syrup-and-pumpkin-seed fudge."

Lisa gave a sudden yell. "Archie!"

Archie, the little sneak, had both his front paws on the counter and was gently removing the opened bar of butter, holding a corner of the paper in his teeth. I grabbed him and ripped the butter away from him before it disappeared into his mouth.

"Bad dog!" I scolded him.

He just wagged his tail. He didn't even look guilty.

"Now, where were we?" I said. "Oh, right, pumpkin seeds."

We went back to work. Things were complicated by the fact that we had no clue what we were doing. The procedure involved some screaming and a lot of laughing. But at last, an hour later, we had two panfuls of a vaguely fudge-like substance.

"Want to taste it?" asked Lisa.

"You first," I said.

"No, you."

We both took tiny pieces and bit into them at the same time.

"Interesting," I said.

"Different," said Lisa.

I gave the rest of my piece to Archie. He would eat anything.

"Maybe Pete would like to try a piece," said Lisa, looking brave. "We need another opinion."

"I think you should take him some," I suggested blandly. "He likes fudge."

Lisa blushed. "Okay," she said. She took several deep breaths as she put a few pieces on a plate. "Here I go. Wait, do I look okay?"

"You look great."

"No, I have to take my hair down." She unpinned her braids, let them down, and shook her hair loose.

"Now I'm ready," she said. She headed upstairs.

I listened as the drumming stopped for about three beats.

In two minutes, she was back down the stairs again.

"Well, what happened?" I asked. "Did he say anything?"

She looked depressed. "Yeah," she said. "He said, 'Uh, thanks, um—' He doesn't even know my name!"

"I'm sure he knows your name," I said. "He's just concentrating on his playing, that's all."

"He doesn't know my name. He doesn't know I exist. I could *die*. I love him!"

"Why?" I said.

"You're his sister. You can't see him the way I see him."

"Right. I see him better."

"You'll see. You'll be in love someday. Then you'll know what I'm going through."

We packed up the fudge. "How much should we charge for this?" I wondered.

"Maybe we should pay them to take it," said Lisa.

The next day we set up our table at school again, and made a new sign. FUDGE FOR FUND-RAISING, 50 CENTS, it said. Underneath, in smaller letters, it said, *What will you eat to save a poor homeless animal?* This sign was Abby's brilliant marketing idea.

The word spread pretty fast about our unusual fudge. We were mobbed with kids, eating fudge and making awful faces.

"This is horrible!" said Matt Barkley.

"Yes, it is," Abby agreed. "But aren't you willing to suffer to save a suffering animal?"

"Yeah, sure." He took something out of his mouth. "What is this, a *pumpkin seed?*"

"Shhh," said Lisa. "Secret recipe."

The fudge flew off our table, and in half an hour there were only two pieces left. We had $52.50.

"Unbelievable," said Lisa. "That sign was pure genius, Abby."

"Let's save these two pieces," I said. "I did promise Miss Hanson we'd bring some over to her house. She got out of the hospital today."

"As long as we warn her," said Lisa. "We don't want to send her back to the hospital."

Molly suggested we drop the money off at the animal shelter afterward, and we all agreed.

We walked over to Miss Hanson's house. It was drizzling a little, and kind of raw and chilly. We walked fast.

Miss Hanson opened the door. She looked pale and a little worn-out, but she was standing straight as ever in a crisp wool bathrobe with white trim around the collar. "How nice to see you girls," she said. "Thank you for taking such good care of Sebastian."

We introduced Abby to her. She knew Abby by sight because she only lived two houses away. "Oh, you're the girl who's always leaving home at five o'clock in the morning, in the pitch dark," she said. "I've often wondered what gets you out of the house so early."

"Gymnastics practice," said Abby.

"Admirable dedication," said Miss Hanson. "Very unusual." The rest of us squirmed, feeling very undedicated and usual.

"Where's Sebastian?" I asked. "Usually he's right here as soon as we walk in the door."

Miss Hanson's face clouded. "Actually, I'm rather worried about him." She led us into the kitchen, where Sebastian was curled up on a mat on the floor. He hardly looked up when he saw us.

"What's wrong with him?" I asked.

"I don't know," she replied. "When I got home, I felt bad for him because he'd been cooped up, so I let him out. When he came back, about an hour later, he seemed very strange. He just went and lay down, and hasn't gotten up since. He's not interested in his food, either. I'm sure he was fine when I got home—he was playing and having fun."

"Golly," Lisa said. "I wonder if something happened to him outside."

"Maybe he ate something he shouldn't have," said Molly.

I looked out Miss Hanson's kitchen window. I could see Mrs. Gresham's living room window from there.

I saw an indistinct figure in the window. Then the curtain dropped, and she was gone.

Trouble Finds Sebastian

The next day, Saturday, I got another call from Miss Hanson at nine o'clock.

"Eliza, I'm wondering if you can help me. I think Sebastian is very sick, and I can't leave the house yet. I'm not even supposed to be out of bed. I was awake with him all night. Could you possibly pick him up and let your mother have a look at him?"

"Of course!" I said.

I threw on my jeans and a sweatshirt. Saturday morning is a busy time for my mom, and she was in the office already. I knew I'd have to stop there and ask if she could squeeze Sebastian in.

I was just walking out the door when the phone rang. It was Lisa.

"I can't talk now," I said. "I have to go pick up Sebastian and take him to my mother. He's really sick."

"I'll be right there. I'll meet you at Miss Hanson's."

My mother said of course she could fit Sebastian in, and I ran down the block to Miss Hanson's. I met Lisa on the way.

"What do you think is the matter with him?" she said.

"I don't have any idea. I'm hoping my mother will figure it out."

When we got to Miss Hanson's, Sebastian was in pretty much the same position he'd been in yesterday. "His stomach's a mess," said Miss Hanson. "*He's* a mess."

"We'll get him fixed up," I said, scooping his limp little body up right along with his red sock. "My mom is the best. She'll figure it out."

I asked Miss Hanson if she needed anything from the store, and she thanked me and said she was fine. Lisa and I said goodbye to her. I tucked Sebastian inside my jacket because it was still drizzling, and we hurried down the street to my mother's office.

My mother was just finishing up with a Great Dane when we got there. He strode through the waiting room like a small horse. A chihuahua yapped ferociously at him as he walked past, and he didn't even turn around to look.

"Come on in, honey," said my mother. Everyone in the waiting room looked daggers at me and Lisa as we went into the examining room.

We put Sebastian on the steel table, where he lay like a limp little noodle. My mother did some basic examining: took his temperature, looked in his ears, felt his belly. He gave a small yelp of pain when she did that.

"He's got a fever," she said. "I think I'm going to have to keep him here until I know what's going on with him. Will you help me take some blood from him?"

I held him still while she took some blood from his leg. I didn't like doing this, but I'd done it a couple of times. Lisa stood near the door, looking about as sick as Sebastian.

"I may need some X-rays, too," my mother said. "First I'll wait and see what the blood work says." She petted him gently, and he purred a little bit. "Why don't you girls go and tell Miss Hanson I'm keeping Sebastian here and that I should know what's wrong with him in a day or two. I'll put him in the back now." She scooped him up and took him to the room in the back with the cages.

Lisa and I fretted and fretted all the way back to Miss Hanson's. What was the matter with Sebastian? Would he die? Had we done something to make him sick while we were taking care of him?

Miss Hanson was calmer about the whole thing than we were. "Sebastian's not going to give up the ghost so easily," she said. "He's too much of a troublemaker. Got too much life in him. He'll be fine, you'll see." We didn't know if she was just putting on an act to calm *us* down or if she really believed it. Either way, it was certain that Miss Hanson had not gotten through life by being a wimp.

We told her we'd come by tomorrow with any news there was about Sebastian. She asked if we'd pick her up some milk, bread, and chamomile tea before we came, and gave us the money for it. We promised to be back by about noon.

As we left, I glanced over at Mrs. Gresham's house. She wasn't in the window.

"Well, what should we do now?" Lisa said as we walked down the street through the drizzle, our heads pulled into our collars like turtles. "I don't really want to go home. I'll just sit around and worry about Sebastian."

"Why don't we see if Abby and Molly are home? We should tell them about Sebastian."

We tried Abby's house first, because it was right there. Her father answered the door. He looked a little surprised to see us—it seemed obvious that he wasn't used to kids coming by for Abby.

We didn't know too much about Abby's father. We knew that she lived alone with him, and we knew that he had once been a gymnast himself. He had almost gone all the way to the Olympics.

We introduced ourselves and asked if Abby was home.

"She's here," he said, "but she's getting physical therapy for her knee. I guess you could come in and talk to her, though." He held the door open for us.

He led us through the living room and downstairs to the finished basement. "Abby," he called. "You've got company."

Abby was sitting on a padded table, and a very strong woman was kneeling in front of her. Abby's face lit up when she saw us. She waved to us. "Hang on a minute," said the woman. "We're almost done with something." She pushed down on Abby's leg, hard, while Abby tried to straighten it.

"Ow!" said Abby.

"Good girl," said the woman. "Just one more time." The woman pushed down, and Abby pushed back again, grunting. There was sweat on her forehead.

All around the room were shelves full of

trophies, and I read the inscriptions on a few that were near me. Some were Abby's for gymnastics. Some were Abby's for horseback riding. And some said, "Jeff Goodman, First Prize in Gymnastics." I guessed that they must have been won by her dad.

"Okay," said the physical therapist to Abby. "That's enough torture for a little while. Why don't you take a short break with your friends?"

"Thanks," said Abby gratefully. She hopped off the table.

"I'm trying to get my knee back in shape so I can compete again in a couple of weeks," she explained to us. "Myra just looks scary. She's really nice."

"No, I'm really scary," said Myra, pouring herself a glass of water.

Abby, Lisa, and I sat down on the sofa. "So, what's going on?" Abby asked.

"We just came by to tell you that Sebastian's sick," I said. "Lisa and I took him over to my mother's this morning, and she's going to keep him and do tests on him."

"He's really in bad shape," said Lisa. "He's so sick!" Her voice quivered a little; she was really scared.

"Oh, no!" said Abby. "What does your mother say?"

"She won't know until she gets the tests back."

"Does Molly know yet?"

"No, we're going to her house after this."

"Can I come too?" said Abby.

"No, you can't," said Myra. "Not until we've done another half hour of therapy, anyhow."

Abby's face fell. "I guess you guys have to leave, huh?" she said to us.

We looked at each other. "Well—" I said.

"I *guess* I could hang around," said Lisa. "I can do my homework later."

"So can I," I said.

"That's so great!" said Abby. "Thanks!"

She hopped back onto the table and we watched her work at her physical therapy for another half hour. It made us understand a lot better that Abby's gymnastics is not just fooling around. This was real "no pain, no gain" stuff.

Finally they were done. "See you on Monday," said Myra, packing up her things.

Abby grabbed her jacket, and we headed upstairs. "Dad, I'm going out with Lisa and Eliza, " Abby called into the kitchen.

"That's fine, Abby," he called back. "Don't get back too late to do a little work with the arm weights."

She sighed. "Okay, Dad."

It had finally stopped drizzling, so our walk over to Molly's wasn't bad. There was a wet wind blowing our hair around.

"So," I said to Abby, "your dad was in the Olympics?"

"Well, he was *almost* in the Olympics. He had to stop because his father died suddenly and he had to go to work. He was the oldest, and my grandmother had three younger kids at home."

"That must have been such a drag for him," I said.

"I think it really was. He never got to find out if he could win a gold medal. I think that's why he pushes me so hard: he wants me to find out how far I can go. Or maybe *he* just wants to find out how far I can go."

"Do you really like competing in gymnastics just for yourself?" I asked her.

She nodded hard. "I love it," she said. "I think that's why I'm good at it. So it's okay that he pushes me, because I push myself too."

Then Lisa waded right in and asked the question I never would have dared to ask: "Where's your mother?"

Abby turned a deep red. "She—lives someplace else," she said.

I knew that this was one mystery we weren't going to find out the answer to anytime soon. Even just-do-it Lisa knew she had crossed the line.

"Sorry," she said. "I'm nosy."

"It's okay," said Abby.

And that was that.

Luckily, we were just getting to Molly's house, so the awkward silence didn't last too long.

Molly was home polishing her mother's silverware. She has to do all the silver about twice a year. She also has to dust all the little china figurines and bowls and candy dishes every week. Molly's house is crammed full of the stuff. Her mother is nuts for doodads.

We told Molly what had happened with Sebastian. She was just as freaked out as the rest of us were.

"Do you think maybe we could go over to your mom's office and visit him?" she asked.

"I guess we could," I said. "If we don't get in her way."

Molly left a note for her mother, who was at work, and we all trooped over to my house. My mother's waiting room was even fuller than it had been before. There wasn't anyplace left to sit. And everybody looked in an even worse mood than the earlier group.

Thank goodness, Eloise was back at work. I went over to her desk and asked her if we could sneak into the back room and visit Sebastian.

"I'll tell you what," she said. "Next time your mom comes out between patients, ask her if you can go back there. I'm sure it would be okay."

In about five minutes, my mother came out. When she saw us in the corner, she beckoned us into the office. More dirty looks from everybody in the waiting room.

"You can go visit him," she said when we were in her examining room, "but don't expect much. I'll tell you, I've been keeping an eye on him, and I took a look at his blood under the microscope, and I'm darned if it doesn't look like he's been poisoned."

Stalking the Culprit

Our four jaws dropped as one.

Poisoned! Sebastian! How could that be? Who would do such a thing? Who would be so—

I saw Lisa and Abby's eyes meet, and Lisa's eyes narrowed. "Mrs. Gresham," she said.

"Whoa, girls," my mother said. "Back up. Let's not go accusing people. There are lots of ways an animal can get poisoned. It can eat a plant with pesticide on it, it can eat poison that's been put down to kill rats, or it can just find something toxic in the garbage. There doesn't have to be a *person* behind it."

"But there *could* be a person behind it," said Lisa darkly.

"What kind of poison was it?" Abby asked.

"I don't know yet," my mother replied. "I have to wait for all the lab work to come back. I'm not even sure it *is* poison yet."

"Mom, do you think he's going to be okay?" I asked her.

"I can't know that yet, honey. It depends on what's wrong with him, and how bad it is. You know I'll do my level best to save him."

"Can we see him?" said Molly.

"Sure," said my mother. "Just don't pester him."

We all went into the back room. Sebastian seemed about the same as before: miserable. He was lying on his side, panting, and his eyes were dull. We talked to him for a couple of minutes, but he wasn't interested.

"Do you feel better now that you've seen him?" I asked Molly as we walked out.

"No, worse," she said.

We said goodbye to my mother. "Try not to worry, girls," she said. "I have lots of tricks up my sleeve."

When we were out on the street, we just stood there. "What should we do now?" Abby asked.

"Let's go make a citizen's arrest of Mrs. Gresham," said Abby.

"A what?" I said.

"A citizen's arrest. My dad told me about it once. You can just arrest somebody if you know they did a crime."

"But we don't even know she did anything!" I said. "And besides, what are we going to do with her after we arrest her? Lock her up in your basement?"

Molly was looking down the street. "Hey, look!" she broke in. "There she goes!"

There went Mrs. Gresham in the flesh, all right. She was heading the other way, pushing a folding shopping cart. She had on a frilly lavender dress and a big floppy hat, and about forty pounds of bracelets.

"She must be going shopping on that big street," said Lisa. "The one with all the stores, about four blocks away? I can never remember names of streets."

"Commonwealth Avenue," said Molly.

"Right," said Lisa.

"Let's follow her," said Abby.

"Yeah!" said Lisa. "Let's see where she goes."

"We can see if she buys any poison," said Abby.

"Oh, like sure," I said, "she's going to the poison store to buy a big brown bottle with a skull and crossbones on it."

"You never know," said Lisa. "Come on."

We headed down the street after Mrs. Gresham, rushing until we got about half a block behind her. Then we just walked along at her slow pace.

"I've never followed anybody before," I whispered. "I feel so *weird!*"

"What if she turns around and sees us?" said Molly.

"So what?" said Lisa. "We have a right to walk on the street too."

When we got to Commonwealth Avenue, she slowed down. She stopped at every store window, frowning at the merchandise on display. Finally she went into the supermarket.

"Great," said Lisa. "It's big. It'll be easy to follow her in there."

I cleared my throat. "I think I hear—"

"—Your mother calling you," said Lisa.

"I'm not going in there," I said. "You can go if you want to. I'm too scared."

"Okay, you stay out here and we'll go in," said Abby.

They all went in after Mrs. Gresham, and I peeked in between two sale posters that were taped onto the plate glass window of the store. I could only see one aisle this way; if I wanted to follow all the action, I'd have to hop back and forth between the ads for yogurt and bread and broccoli, peering between the cracks.

I got her in my sights pretty quickly, in the spaghetti aisle. I could tell she was one of those people who goes shopping for entertainment. She went up and down the aisles, picking up lots of things, reading the labels, shaking her head, rattling and knocking packages. It would have been obvious to any stranger observing her that this woman did not have a life.

I watched my friends hang behind her, ready to flee if she turned in their direction. But she never did. In real life, it seemed, it was amazingly easy to follow somebody. You didn't have to dart around and flatten yourself against walls at all. I'd have to remember this in case I wanted to be a private detective instead of a vet when I grew up.

Mrs. Gresham yelled at a stockboy. He stopped what he was doing and got her a box of cereal from a top shelf. Then she decided she didn't want to buy it and made him put it back. Then she yelled at the mother of a very cute toddler who was standing in the middle of the aisle. Then she bashed her cart into a large cardboard store display and sent about a thousand little boxes of crackers tumbling to the floor. She kept on walking and didn't even look back.

At last, she was done shopping. Lisa and Abby stayed in the produce section and pushed Molly toward the checkout counters. I had to hop madly from one gap to the next to see both Mrs. Gresham and Molly.

Luckily, Mrs. Gresham picked the last line on the left, so Molly could spy on her from behind without her seeing.

All I could see was that Mrs. Gresham put three items onto the conveyor belt. One of them was a package of hamburger. I couldn't tell what the others were.

Molly was not a natural spy. She looked like she was in pain. But she was doing her job: she was watching Mrs. Gresham's purchases carefully. She winced when Mrs. Gresham yelled at the cashier for something or other.

As soon as Molly was sure she had seen it all, she got out of there, rushing back to Lisa and Abby. I watched as Mrs. Gresham paid, counting out the money penny by penny into the cashier's hand. When she started walking out, I ran in a panic for the entryway of the florist next door.

After about two minutes, I got up the nerve to peek. Molly, Abby, and Lisa were spilling out of the supermarket, giggling hysterically and shushing each other. I ran back to them.

"Where is she?" Lisa asked in a loud whisper.

We looked around. There she was, two doors down, squinting suspiciously into a window.

"What'd she buy in the supermarket?" I whispered to Molly.

Molly the spy hardly moved her lips as she talked. "Hamburger. Canned asparagus. Canned spinach."

"*Eeeew*," we all whispered at once. "Disgusting."

"What did she yell at the cashier about?" Abby asked Molly.

"She had a coupon from 1979 and the cashier said she couldn't take it."

"The hamburger," said Lisa, "could be to put the poison in."

"Wait. She's going into the hardware store," said Abby.

The hardware store was too small for all of us to go into without being seen.

"Who's going in this time?" Abby whispered.

"Eliza's turn," Lisa giggled, and she shoved me in the door. Before I could protest, I was inside.

My knees were knocking. I saw Mrs. Gresham disappear down the paint aisle. I ducked into the doorknob-and-hinge aisle and tried to look like a doorknob.

I hung around there for a few minutes, waiting for her to go up to the front, wondering where she was. Then I felt the hairs at the back of my neck prickle. I turned around slowly. She was standing right behind me.

I gasped, but she just kept walking toward me.

"*Excuse* me," she said. "You're taking up the whole aisle."

"S-s-sorry," I stammered.

She peered at me for a minute, as if she were trying to place my face. Then she just shook her head and kept going up to the front. I managed to see that she was carrying a large bottle of rose food. She went up to the counter in front, and I scooted out the door, trying to be as invisible as possible. I don't think she saw me as she paid for it penny by penny.

"Let's go!" I yelled to my friends outside the store. "She's about to come out and she almost recognized me."

We all ran to the shoe store at the end of the block because the front door was way inside, off the sidewalk. I started fake-beating-up Lisa. "How could you do that to me?" I yelled.

"Do you think she knew you were following her?" Abby asked.

"No, she just thought I was in her way, I'm pretty sure."

"Thank goodness!" said Lisa. "What did she buy in there?"

"Rose food. No poison."

"Look!" said Molly. "She's going into the drugstore across the street."

"The drugstore!" said Lisa. "She could be buying poison in there for sure."

"Guys, I don't think we should keep following her around," I said. "What if we get caught? Isn't it a crime or something? Mrs. Gresham is always looking for a reason to call the police!"

"Let's just do this one last store," said Lisa. "I'll go this time. She won't figure it out."

"Okay," I said. "But I'm not going anyplace near there."

"Why don't you guys start walking home?" Lisa suggested. "I'll catch up, or I'll meet you at Eliza's, okay? That way we don't have to worry about being seen."

"Okay," I said, relieved to be getting out of there.

When Mrs. Gresham was safely inside the drugstore, Lisa darted across the street and into the store. I prayed that Mrs. Gresham wouldn't see her, remember that she'd seen her with me, and start wondering. But then again, I thought, why would she? We weren't together, as far as she knew. And why should she think we were following her?

Unless, I thought, she was guilty and she knew we were onto her.

Abby, Molly, and I walked slowly down the street toward my house. I was afraid to look behind us. But finally, when we were almost at my house, Lisa came pounding up.

"She went home the other way," she panted. "She didn't see me. We're safe."

"What'd she get at the drugstore?" Abby asked.

"Heartburn medicine. I stood on line right behind her so I could see. I had to buy some bubblegum. Want some?" Lisa passed the pack around.

We all took some gum and chewed madly. I think we were getting the tension out of our systems.

"Heartburn medicine!" I snorted. "That's perfect. I bet she gets heartburn all the time. Doesn't she look like a heartburn type?"

"Definitely," Molly agreed.

"So what did we learn from our little spying trip, anyway?" I said. "We didn't see her buy any poison. All we know is that she has heartburn, grows roses, and eats horrible food."

"I still think she did it," said Lisa.

"She could have," said Abby. "I live next to her, and I know she's capable of practically anything."

"I don't think she would do something like poison a cat," said Molly. "I think she just likes to be rude and mean. She's too chicken to do something really awful."

"I'm with Molly," I said.

"You guys have too much faith," said Lisa. "She did it. You'll see."

Sebastian Finds
More Trouble

My mother took care of Sebastian practically around the clock, and by Tuesday he was doing a little better. He wasn't eating yet, but at least he picked his head up. I visited him whenever I could.

Miss Hanson was also doing better. She was getting stronger and looking healthier, and by Tuesday afternoon she was able to walk over to my mother's office and visit Sebastian. I happened to be there when she got there.

"There you are, you little troublemaker," said Miss Hanson, looking genuinely relieved to see him.

"He's not completely out of danger yet," said my mother, "but he's getting there. If he keeps improving, I think he should be out of the woods by tomorrow or Thursday."

"Have you figured out what's wrong with him?" Miss Hanson asked her.

"I got the lab results back, finally. He's ingested a small amount of rat poison. It's actually rather an unusual kind, not used much anymore. It's called TDZ."

"Good Lord," said Miss Hanson.

I couldn't tell whether she was thinking about Mrs. Gresham or not, and I certainly wasn't going to ask.

I got a late start to school the next morning, and I was walking fast down Neptune when I saw Molly up ahead. She and I were tardy a lot, and sometimes we had to go to the office together and get notes. Neither one of us was good for much in the morning.

"Hey, Molly! Wait up!" I yelled. She turned, yawning, and I ran to catch up.

"Guess what?" she said.

"What?" I panted.

"I did a little research at the library yesterday afternoon, and guess what I found out?"

"What?" I panted again.

"The *city* put out rat poison about a week and a half ago. It was in the newspaper. It seems there were a lot of rats down by the wharves, and they decided to get rid of them. They put signs up all around there for pet owners, saying not to let them loose. I think that maybe Sebastian, being a cat, went down there, caught a rat or a mouse that had eaten the poison, and got sick himself."

"Did the article say what kind of rat poison it was?"

"Yup, it was something with initials...let's see, it was TDZ," said Molly of the great memory.

"That's it!" I whooped. "That's what my mother says is making him sick!"

"There we are then. I guess this proves that Mrs. Gresham didn't poison him."

"I guess so," I said, feeling some relief that the mystery was solved.

The rest of the week went by very fast. By Saturday, Sebastian was up and around, and my mother declared him fit to go home.

Miss Hanson came to pick him up, and Molly, Lisa, and I met her at the office and walked her back to her house. Abby was having physical therapy again. The three of us took turns carrying Sebastian in his pet carrier. He meowed piteously the whole way.

"I guess he's feeling better if he wants to get out of there so badly," Miss Hanson said.

It was a good thing we were getting Sebastian home that morning, because a big storm was coming on. The sky was turning darker and darker.

When we got to Miss Hanson's house, we put the carrier down on the living room floor and opened it up. Out stepped Sebastian, looking a little wary. He started walking around the room sniffing things, until he was satisfied that nothing had changed in his absence. He looked a lot thinner.

But when he found his little catnip mouse, he suddenly became the old Sebastian. He pounced on it, threw it up in the air, and pounced on it again. We all breathed a quiet sigh of relief as we watched him.

"Would you girls like a cup of chamomile tea?" Miss Hanson asked.

"Okay," we all said. It was nice having tea with Miss Hanson. We felt very grown-up doing it.

She put the kettle on and we sat down at her kitchen table and watched Sebastian play. "I'll just see if my mail came," she said. Sebastian followed her.

A moment later we heard her yell. "Sebastian, come back here!"

We ran to the front door, already knowing what had happened. Sebastian had slipped out when she'd opened the door.

A deep rumble of thunder sounded in the

distance. "We'd better go find him before the storm starts," I said.

"Maybe he'll find his way home," said Miss Hanson, looking a bit worried.

"If there's a bad storm, he'll get all confused and scared," said Lisa. "I think we should go out and get him."

Miss Hanson turned the teakettle off, and we put our jackets on. "We'll see you later," I said.

"Thank you, girls," she said. "That cat is a world of trouble."

"That's why we love him," said Lisa.

Crisis on the Cliffs

We stood on the sidewalk in front of Miss Hanson's house and looked as far as we could see in both directions. No Sebastian.

"He's probably right in Mrs. Gresham's yard, ripping up her rosebushes," said Molly.

We ran back to look, but he wasn't there.

"Let's check the neighborhood," I said.

We decided to head toward Commonwealth Avenue, because we didn't want him ending up on a big street with all those cars. Walking fast, we craned our necks into all the yards, yelling for Sebastian. There was a sudden clap of thunder that startled us.

"How far do you think we should go before we turn around and try another direction?" Lisa said.

"Let's just go as far as Commonwealth," I said. "Then we'll try someplace else."

We kept going, calling all the time. The

sky by this time had turned a sickening shade of greenish-black.

About half a block from Commonwealth, we bumped into Abby. "Hi, guys, what's up?" she said.

"We're searching for Sebastian," I said. "He got loose again."

"Oh, no," she said. "I'll help you look for him. Where are you trying?"

"We figured we'd go as far as Commonwealth," Lisa said, "and then we'd go someplace else. I think maybe we should try down by the water. If he did go down there before, then maybe he likes it there."

"You know, it's funny," said Abby. "I just bumped into Mrs. Gresham. I'm supposed to exercise my knee, and I was taking a walk down by the cliffs. She was heading down there in a big hurry. She was carrying a cardboard box."

"How big was it?" Lisa asked slowly.

"It was about like this..." Abby showed us with her hands. The box she was making in the air was just about Sebastian-sized.

We just stood there letting this information sink in.

"Let's go!" said Lisa.

We started running for the cliffs, as a huge crack of lightning flashed, followed almost immediately by a boom of thunder.

"If my mother knew I was out in this, she'd kill me," said Molly.

As we ran, I kept calling for Sebastian, just in case it wasn't him in the box. But he didn't turn up, because of course it was him in the box.

"I *knew* it. I *knew* she was bad news. I bet she poisoned him, too," said Lisa.

"She's going to throw him right into the ocean if we don't stop her!" cried Abby.

"We don't know anything for sure yet," I panted, starting to run out of breath. This was because I stood around in gym whenever I possibly could.

"Let's turn left here," said Abby. "She looked like she was heading for Cannon Cove."

We tore around the corner and headed for Cannon Cove, which was named that because when the tide comes in, it makes a huge booming noise like a cannon. Tourists come to see it in the summer.

A fine rain had begun to fall. In a couple of minutes, we knew, it would be pouring.

As we got to the head of the cliffs, we could just make out a figure through the rain, a figure that seemed to be weaving and swaying in the distance. We moved closer, and then we heard that unmistakable voice. It was Mrs. Gresham.

"Help! Help!" she was yelling, and waving her arms around like a demented scarecrow.

We sprinted over to her.

"Help!" she repeated.

"What happened?" I shouted over the thunder.

"The cat! He's gone!"

"What did you do?" shouted Lisa bitterly.

"I only meant to scare him and teach Hanson a lesson," she whimpered. "He came straight for my rosebushes again today, and I've had enough. I was going to lock him in that shed for the night—" She pointed to a ramshackle shed at the top of the cliffs. It had once been used for storing lobster pots, but nobody has been in it for years. "But when I took him out of the box he jumped out of my arms and ran down there!" We followed her eyes right over the cliffs, and we gasped. "I called him, but of course he wouldn't come to me."

"Did he fall?" I shouted.

"No. He just ran down the cliffs and got himself stuck in one of those caves down there. And now I can't get him out!" she wailed in terror. "I only wanted to scare him, I didn't want to really hurt him! He was just

97

going to be locked in for the night—" She started blubbering, sending her mascara running in streams down her face.

My father had always told me that the more of a bully somebody is, the more of a chicken they really are deep down. I just hadn't known that the rule applied to nasty old ladies just as much as to large mean boys at recess.

"Which cave is he in?" Lisa demanded.

"I don't know which one. I think it's one of the caves near the bottom."

"The trouble is," shouted Molly over the wind, "that when the tide comes in, it goes way up the cliffs. All those bottom caves fill up with water. If we don't get him out, he might drown!"

"When does the tide come in?" I asked her. This was the kind of thing I counted on her to know.

"I'm not sure—I think in about half an hour, maybe less!"

"Let's go get him!" said Abby.

There are some stairs cut into the side of the cliff, but you have to be careful on them even when it isn't the middle of a thunderstorm. They're all uneven, and some of them are about as high as your knee. There was nothing to do but start down them, very slowly. I was petrified, and my glasses were fogging up.

It was raining harder now. The four of us wended our way down the side of the cliff, while Mrs. Gresham stayed at the top and watched, waving her arms.

Just before we were too far down the cliff to see the top, I looked up one last time. Miss Hanson, dressed in a yellow slicker and rain-hat, was pedaling toward the cliffs on her bicycle. She shouldn't have been out in this! She must have been frantic about Sebastian. I checked my watch. We'd left her house at two, and it was now almost three.

She stopped beside Mrs. Gresham. There was a lot of shouting and gesturing and point-ing, and Miss Hanson looked over the edge at us.

I cupped my hands to my mouth. "Don't worry!" I shouted as loud as I could. "We'll get him!" I couldn't tell if she heard me or not.

By the time we'd climbed all the way to the bottom, the rain and wind were so strong that it looked as if the air was full of blowing smoke. How would we ever find a kitten in this?

There was only a tiny, rocky strip of beach left to walk on. Pretty soon, the tide would cover it all up. We walked along it, yelling "Sebastian! Sebastian!" All we could hear was the roaring of the waves and the wind and the rain.

We kept walking. Our sneakers and socks were soaked and freezing. The waves were starting to hit the cove.

"Listen!" said Lisa.

We all stood and listened.

"I can't hear anything," I said, shaking my head.

"Sshhh," said Lisa.

There was a tiny, tiny mewing. You could just hear it on the wind.

"Where's it coming from?" Abby said.

"There...no, there," said Lisa, pointing. We ran down the beach and stood below a little chink in the rocks—not even a cave, really—that was about eight feet above our heads.

"Sebastian!" yelled Molly.

"Mew!" We heard it again.

"Don't worry, we're coming to get you, Sebastian," called Lisa. We could just see his little face, peeking out over the edge above us.

"How are we going to get up there?" Molly said.

"We'll climb," said Abby. "We can do it. There are some footholds."

"Maybe you should go," I said. "You're a gymnast. You can get up there."

"Okay," said Abby. "I'll try."

We all bit our lips as Abby started climbing up the cliff. Carefully, she would find a foothold and a place to hold on with her hands. Then she would do it again a little higher. "This isn't bad," she called down from about four feet. "You can—*OW!*" Abby's leg crumpled under her, and she came crashing down.

We were all over her in a second: "Abby are you all right?" "What happened?"

She sat up, rubbing her side. "I'm okay," she said through gritted teeth. "It's just my stupid knee. It gave out under me. I'm just a little bruised, that's all."

She stood up to show us that she was all right.

We heard a plaintive yowl from Sebastian. The rain beat down.

"Now what?" I said.

"I'll try it," said Lisa.

Suddenly, an alien took over my body. "No," I heard myself say. "It's not fair for me to let other people take the risks, just because I'm always chicken. I'll try to climb up there."

Something about the tone of my voice

must have sounded serious, because they all just looked at me.

"Okay," said Lisa. "Go for it, Eliza."

So I went for it. I marched up to the side of the cliff, having absolutely no idea how I was going to get up there. *One foot at a time*, I decided. *I'm just going to do it one foot at a time, and I'm not going to look down.*

I looked for a place to put my foot, and found one not too far above me. Grabbing onto some sharp rocks, I hoisted myself up. There. I was a couple of feet off the ground now.

I heard Abby's voice below me. "There's a good place for your foot just to your right!" she was calling.

I looked for it, and found it. Hugging very, very close to the rocks, I climbed up one more step.

"Yaaay, Eliza!" yelled Molly.

"Take a rest if you're tired," Abby called.

"No, I can keep going," I shouted, feeling like Supergirl all of a sudden. I was doing it!

There was another ledge above me, and I went for that. Panic struck as my foot slipped a bit when I put it on the ledge, but I tried it again and it held. The rain was streaming from my hair into my eyes. I wished I had windshield wipers for my glasses.

I kept climbing, following Sebastian's meowing. And then, with one last haul upward, there I was—face to face with one wet, bedraggled, scared kitten.

"Sebastian!" I said. "You little pain!"

I could hear my friends below clapping and cheering. I had done it! I had done something really brave and fearless. Well, no, not fearless—full of fear—but I had done it anyway. That was even better.

I reached out and grabbed him. At least he didn't give me a hard time about that. His fur was totally drenched.

And then I realized I had a problem. I turned around and looked down, which made me so dizzy I almost fell.

"I don't know how to climb down with him!" I screeched.

There was a lot of yelled discussion below me. And then I heard another voice from above.

"Hold on!" it said. It was Mrs. Gresham.

I looked up to see her waving her arms at me. Then she disappeared from the top of the cliff. What on earth could she be doing?

A minute later she reappeared. She was dragging the old wooden ladder that had been leaning up against the side of the shed.

"Get out of the way!" she screamed. "I'm

going to send it down!" She was standing maybe about three stories directly above Abby, Lisa, and Molly.

I didn't think it would be close enough to hit me, but I was still nervous. Abby, Lisa, and Molly jumped out of the way.

"Here goes!" yelled Mrs. Gresham, and she pushed the ladder over the side of the cliff. It slid and clattered all the way to the bottom.

Abby quickly ran over and grabbed it, with Lisa and Molly not far behind. They stood it up below me and held it firm.

"Eliza!" Miss Hanson yelled from above. "Put Sebastian in your shirt!"

I hadn't thought of that. It was a good idea, if he didn't totally claw my stomach in terror.

"Okay, Sebastian," I said firmly. "You're going in my shirt. And you're not going to put your claws out, okay?"

I put the soaking kitten down the front of my soaking shirt, letting his head peek out from between two of the buttons so he wouldn't panic in there. He didn't fight me. I think he knew his rotten little skin was being saved.

I had to hold onto the rocks on the ledge with my hands, while I felt around for the top rung of the ladder with my foot. Then I did the same thing with the next rung, until I could hold onto the ladder and make my way down. Abby, Lisa, and Molly were holding it tight, thank goodness. Slowly, slowly, I made my way down it, until finally I was at the bottom.

More clapping and cheering, and lots of hugging too. Poor Sebastian almost got squashed in the process. I was never so happy to be on the ground as I was at that moment.

Well, it wasn't exactly on the ground. It was in about a foot of water. The cove was filling up fast, and the waves were trying to drag our legs right out from under us. "Let's get out of here!" I yelled.

We turned and ran, or sloshed, for the steps. Sebastian was still peeking out the front of my shirt. Climbing up the steps was actually a little easier than climbing down had been, and it seemed like a perfect breeze to me after my climb up the cliffs to get Sebastian.

When we were about halfway up the steps, we were startled by a huge *BOOM!* Cannon Cove was doing its thing. A tremendous wave had hit the cove, right where we'd been standing three minutes ago. It probably would have swept us all right out to sea. If Sebastian had still been in his cave, it might have sucked him out too.

We scrambled up the last few steps, and we were safe. We ran over to Miss Hanson. I unbuttoned a couple of buttons on my shirt and pulled Sebastian out and handed him to Miss Hanson.

As I buttoned my shirt up again, Miss Hanson held Sebastian to her. I couldn't be sure if I was really seeing her eyes get wet, or if it was just the rain. But her voice shook just a bit as she said, "Thank you. Thank you very much." Then she took a deep breath, squared her shoulders under her yellow raincoat, and held Sebastian up. "You are in big trouble, young man," she said. He actually looked ashamed of himself.

Mrs. Gresham had come running over by this time. "I'm sorry!" she was blubbering. "Believe me, I never meant to hurt him! I just wanted to teach him a lesson!"

"Oh, be quiet, Emily," said Miss Hanson. "You can apologize later. I want to get these kids home and dry them off."

Small Victories

We sat in Miss Hanson's kitchen, wearing an odd assortment of her bathrobes, nightshirts, and flannel pajamas and drinking tea while she dried our clothes in her dryer. After we'd taken hot showers, we had all called our parents, assuming they'd be out of their minds worrying about us, only to find that Molly's mother was the only one who was worried. The rest of them, in their infinite faith in our intelligence, had assumed that we were waiting out the storm snug and dry somewhere.

It was Miss Hanson I was really worried about. She should never have been outside.

"I've been out in plenty worse weather than this," she reassured me, fluffing up an indignant Sebastian with the hair dryer. "I'll be just fine."

"I'm worried about Sebastian, too," said

Lisa. "He's just getting better from being poisoned. He didn't need to be out in that storm either."

"Sebastian's even tougher than me," said Miss Hanson.

"You know," said Molly, stirring her tea slowly, "I was thinking about that poison. The city shouldn't be allowed to put out poison that's going to be so dangerous to pets. I think we should make them stop."

"Are you *positive* Mrs. Gresham didn't poison Sebastian?" Lisa said.

"I'm positive," said Molly. "It was the same stuff the city put out. It's too much of a coincidence."

"I'm sure of it too," said Miss Hanson. "I've known Emily Gresham a long time. She's a pain in the neck, full of hot air, and she likes to make trouble. But she wouldn't kill a kitten."

"To get back to the other point," said Abby, who was sitting on the floor with an ice pack on her knee, "how could we get the city to stop using poison?"

"Well, I've given that some thought," said Molly. Of course she had. "First, I thought I'd do some research at City Hall and see if it's legal for them to do it. Then, I thought I'd do some research at the library and see if there's a different way they could control the rats—one that wouldn't hurt the pets. Then, I thought we'd make up a petition and see if we could get a whole lot of signatures on it. Then, I thought we could get the people from Channel 7 to come and do a story when we present the petition to the city."

"Boy," said Abby, "you sure thought a lot of stuff."

"That's just how I am," said Molly, blushing.

The bell on Miss Hanson's dryer rang, and we all went to get our clothes and go home.

A month passed, and a number of things happened during it:

• Mrs. Gresham bought Sebastian fifty pounds of cat food and apologized to Miss Hanson. Miss Hanson accepted her apology, and they had tea at Miss Hanson's house. Miss Hanson said she'd try to see that Sebastian didn't get out of the house anymore. Mrs. Gresham discovered that she was allergic to Sebastian and sneezed the whole time.

• Molly carried out her entire plan about the rat poison. After doing a lot of research, she decided that the thing to do was to ask the city to put out a lot of traps instead of poison, in places where pets couldn't get to them. She wrote up a petition and made a bunch of copies, and we all went around from house to house getting signatures. We ended up taking 293 signatures to City Hall, and Channel 7 *did* come (it was our old friend James Johnson), and—guess what? The city said "Yes." Just as simple as that. They had been thinking that the poison wasn't so good for the environment anyway.

• Miss Hanson stayed in bed for another couple of weeks, and then she was fine. Sebastian was fine immediately. I, however, got a killer cold.

• Abby's knee took a long time to heal, and her father was pretty mad that she'd tried climbing the cliff. She told him she had to have a life, and friends, and she wasn't sorry she'd done it, and he backed off. A little.

• Sebastian decided he was too old and sophisticated a guy to be sleeping on a red sock, so he just stopped. He started sleeping on Miss Hanson's stereo instead, because he liked the warmth. Miss Hanson washed the sock and gave it to me as a keepsake. "After all," she said, "you saved his life. You're the rightful heir to this sock."

• Molly decided she wanted to take piano lessons from Miss Hanson. After the first lesson, Miss Hanson said she would make a perfectly adequate pianist.

• The fifth grade went on our class trip, having raised enough money. We went to the Statue of Liberty, Ellis Island, and the World Trade Center, and we all had a great time. Only two people threw up on the bus.

• Oh, and I almost forgot. Lisa came to my house and Pete remembered her name.

The Animal Rescue Squad

It was a Friday, one of those freaky, boiling hot days in early June. None of us had much to do after school, so we decided to drop by and see Sebastian. We shuffled toward Miss Hanson's house, made slow and stupid by the heat.

"Things have been kind of boring lately," said Abby. "I miss having some excitement in life."

"You mean, like almost getting killed in Cannon Cove?" I said.

"Well, yeah, sort of," said Abby. "I mean, it was fun. We were doing all these neat things together. Like helping the animal shelter, and taking care of Sebastian, and then saving Sebastian, and doing our rat poison petition. Now what do we do? Just our regular stuff."

The obvious idea was slowly bubbling to

the surface in my brain.

"Guys," I said. "Guys, guys, guys. I have it."

"What do you have?" asked Lisa. "Is it catching?"

"No, I have it. For real."

They all looked at me.

"The Animal Rescue Squad," I said slowly. "A club. Our club. All these things we've been doing are about animals. We all love animals. So let's have a club."

"The Animal Rescue Squad! I love it!" said Lisa.

"It's so, so *official*," Abby said, beaming.

"Maybe we need to incorporate or something," said Molly. "I ought to do some research."

"Molly, we don't need to incorporate!" Lisa yelled cheerfully.

"But we need a handshake or something," I said.

"Yeah, something special, just for us," said Abby.

We had arrived at Miss Hanson's house. We rang the bell, but she wasn't home. Her bicycle was gone from its place in the garage. But we could see Sebastian through the front window, lying on the stereo. He looked at us, blinking sleepily in the heat. He was now a lanky teenager, not a kitten any longer. We rapped on the glass and talked to him. After a couple of minutes of that, we got bored and left.

On the way home, we tried thinking of ideas for a secret handshake or ceremony or flag for the Animal Rescue Squad.

"We could sort of wag our behinds at each other instead of shaking hands," Abby said.

"I don't think so," said Lisa.

"Maybe we could roll over," I said, laughing.

"I don't think so," said Lisa.

"I guess we need to wait for a flash of inspiration," said Molly.

"But with or without a secret thingamajig," said Lisa, "we're still the Animal Rescue Squad from now on, right?"

"Right!" we all said. And right there on the corner of Neptune and Beach, the four of us hugged each other.

Then we decided to all go over to my house and have our first official Animal Rescue Squad meeting, right then and there.

We had just gotten home, and were lounging around the living room petting the dogs, when my mother came in.

"Hi, girls," she said. "What's up?"

I told her all about the Animal Rescue

Squad, and she said she liked the idea. "If you need a consulting veterinarian, I'm always here," she offered. "But no wild animals, okay?"

Abby blushed.

"Would you all like to stay for dinner?" my mother offered. She turned to me. "Your dad's at a meeting, and he won't be home till late. There's plenty of food."

"Mom, could we all have a sleepover?" I begged her. "We won't get too loud, I promise."

"If you help clean up after dinner," she said.

"Deal!"

Dinner was kind of funny. Abby and Molly and I kept laughing at stupid things. And every time Pete looked at Lisa or asked her to pass the salt or the butter, she would drop something.

After dinner, the four of us thundered upstairs to my room to start our Animal Rescue Squad meeting.

My eyes fell on the red Christmas sock, which was draped over the back of my desk chair. "Hey," I said, "maybe we could do something with Sebastian's sock."

"I think it's our secret thingamajig," said Molly.

"Yes!" said Lisa. "The Sacred Red Sock!"

We all nodded gravely. The Sacred Red Sock. It was just right.

"It could be kind of like a flag for the Animal Rescue Squad," Abby suggested.

"I know, I know!" I said. "When there's a problem for the Squad to solve, or when we need a meeting or something, we'll hang the Sacred Red Sock out the window."

"Okay," said Lisa. "How about this. Everybody gets the Sacred Red Sock for a month. Whoever has the Sock is the leader of the Animal Rescue Squad for that month."

"Great," I said.

"Perfect," said Abby.

"And I'll take the minutes at our meetings," Molly offered.

"Take the minutes? What does that mean?" Abby asked.

"It means I write down what happens at our meetings. So we have a record."

"So there it is!" said Lisa. "This is our first official meeting of the Animal Rescue Squad."

"Maybe you should call the meeting to order, Eliza," said Molly. "You're the first Keeper of the Sock." It was draped across my lap at that moment.

"Okay," I said, taking a deep breath. "The

first meeting of the Animal Rescue Squad is hereby called to order."

"What should we talk about?" said Lisa.

I knitted my brows. "Hmmm," I ruminated. "Let's see...does anybody have any news to report?" I asked.

"I think the animal shelter's doing a lot better," Lisa reported.

"That's great," said Abby.

"I heard somebody died and left them twenty thousand dollars," said Molly. "My mother said it was on the news."

"That's so great!" I said.

"I talked to the lady who took Bandit, my little raccoon," said Abby. "She said he grew like crazy and was really smart. She had a hard time not getting too attached to him. By last week he was ready to be let out in the woods. She's sure he's going to be fine."

I was really glad that story had had a happy ending.

That was it for the news. Molly was busily writing all of it down in her notebook, on a page with "A.R.S. Minutes" printed on the top.

"Do we have any money in our treasury?" I asked. "We could talk about things to do with it."

"No money," said Lisa. "But we do have a

priceless recipe for Pumpkin Seed Fudge."

We all snorted and made gagging noises.

"If we do get any money, do you want to be the treasurer?" I asked her.

"Sure," she said.

"Do we have any plans?" I asked the group.

We all looked at each other.

"No plans, I guess," I said.

"I guess we'll just deal with crisis situations as they come up," said Molly.

Everyone nodded sagely.

"Anything else?" I asked.

Abby yawned. "I'm kind of sleepy. I had to get up at five to practice this morning."

The yawn was contagious. Molly yawned, then Lisa, then me. Even Archie, who was lying at the foot of the bed chewing on a squeaky toy, yawned.

"I guess the Animal Rescue Squad's first meeting is hereby finished," I said.

Everybody agreed. And then the Animal Rescue Squad went to sleep.

Don't miss the next book in
The Animal Rescue Squad series:
THE ANIMAL RESCUE SQUAD #2
Hand-Me-Down Chimp

Gumbo made his move. He made a tremendous flying leap off the top of the bookcase and landed on the chandelier that hung in the middle of the room. The little hanging drops of glass tinkled as he swung there, and I prayed that the whole thing didn't fall down. My grandmother had momentarily stopped yelling to watch in horror. I could hear Eliza behind me, mumbling, "Ai-yi-yi. Ai-yi-yi."

"Gumbo," I said. "Come down. Come to Lisa." I put my arms out to him.

But Gumbo wasn't coming down.

About the Authors

ELLEN WEISS and MEL FRIEDMAN are a husband-and-wife team who have written many popular books for young readers, including *The Curse of the Calico Cat*, *The Adventures of Ratman*, *The Tiny Parents*, and *The Poof Point*.

They live in New York with their daughter, Nora, and their boxer, Gracie. Over the years they have taken in many stray animals, among them dogs named Big, Little, and Archie.

You've met Eliza, Lisa, Molly, and Abby...
Now meet the girls at the

Jina, Andie, Laurie, and Mary Beth—the four roommates in Suite 4B at Foxhall Academy— may not see eye to eye on everything. But they do agree on one thing: they *love* horses! You'll want to read all the books in this extra-special series.